Praise for Jess Michaels's
Pleasuring the Lady

"...a tantalizing take on the forced marriage trope that will leave readers breathless and wishing for more!"
~ *RT Book Reviews*

"...a heady tale of dangerous passions, damaging lies and true, abiding love...that will delight longtime fans and new readers alike."
~ *The Romance Reviews*

"A historical that will have you looking at history in a totally different way...an awesome love story..."
~ *Night Owl Reviews*

"Once again Jess Michaels has delivered a lovely, romantic tale full of emotion and erotic pleasure. A must read for historical romance lovers."
~ *Fiction Vixen Book Reviews*

"...an extraordinary, sensuous, tantalizing romance..."
~ *Unwrapping Romance*

"I really enjoyed *Pleasuring the Lady*...Jess Michaels writes exceptional historical romance filled with strong emotional characters, passion, and erotic pleasures."
~ *Fresh Fiction*

Look for these titles by
Jess Michaels

Now Available:

Mistress Matchmaker
An Introduction to Pleasure
For Desire Alone
Her Perfect Match

The Pleasure Wars
Taken by the Duke
Pleasuring the Lady
Beauty and the Earl
Beautiful Distraction

The Ladies Book of Pleasures
A Matter of Sin
A Moment of Pleasure
A Measure of Deceit

Pleasuring the Lady

Jess Michaels

SAMHAIN PUBLISHING

Samhain Publishing, Ltd.
11821 Mason Montgomery Road, 4B
Cincinnati, OH 45249
www.samhainpublishing.com

Pleasuring the Lady
Copyright © 2013 by Jess Michaels
Print ISBN: 978-1-61922-205-2
Digital ISBN: 978-1-61921-751-5

Editing by Amy Sherwood
Cover by Kim Killion

First Samhain Publishing, Ltd. electronic publication: November 2013
First Samhain Publishing, Ltd. print publication: November 2014

Dedication

For Michael. Thanks for supporting the "family business" and assisting me in the difficult task of maintaining sanity in an insane industry.

Chapter One

Portia settled back on the settee and smiled as her friend Ava, who had been the Duchess of Rothcastle for nearly half a year, gushed with great enthusiasm about her life.

"Oh, I've been going on and on," Ava said, at last pausing for breath and blushing deeply when she saw her friend's amused expression. "I'm so sorry!"

Portia laughed softly at her friend's utterly unnecessary apology.

"After so many years of comparing sad stories in the corners of ballrooms, do you think I would not wish to hear all the details of your joy? There is no one else in the world that deserves happiness as much as you do."

"Except you," Ava said with a smile.

Portia tried to leave the same expression on her face, though her friend's playful comment brought her no pleasure. Portia no longer had great expectations about a love-filled life to gush over as her friend now did. She tried not to think about that impossible future, to long for it, anymore.

She waved her hand in the hopes she could change the subject. "Who would have thought when the Season began last year that you would end up married to...*happily* married to...your family's greatest enemy? What a world we live in, where anything can change in a moment!"

Ava nodded, but a tortured darkness entered her gaze. "*Almost* anything can change. Some things have not. Or have changed for the worse."

Portia flinched, for there was no doubt to what...or whom...her friend referred.

She drew a short breath before she asked what was sure to be a painful question. And not just for Ava.

"Have you heard from your brother?"

Ava struggled to keep her composure for a moment, but Portia knew her friend too well not to see the slight tremble to her lip, the swelling of tears in her eyes, the paling of her skin.

"No," she finally whispered. "Not since he disappeared as soon as he knew Christian and I were departing for Gretna Green. So it has been over six months."

Portia shook her head. "I had hoped at Christmas—"

Ava shoved to her feet. "Yes. So had I. But there was no word, not even a one-line wish to make merry for the holiday." The tears her friend had been fighting began to fall now. "It seems Liam has cut me off entirely. It is the only source of pain in all my recent happiness."

Portia stood and crossed to wrap her arms around her friend. Her heart swelled with pity for Ava, for she knew how much her friend cared for her wayward brother. And she felt for Liam too. He had hated Ava's new husband for so long, it must have broken him to see her seduced by and ultimately wed to him.

She could only imagine his pain. How she wished she could comfort him. Not that he would allow it from *her*, a person he probably never thought about.

"I'm so sorry," Portia whispered, shoving thoughts of Liam away. Her friend needed her, she had to concentrate.

"It is even worse," Ava sobbed. "I heard not two days ago that he is in London. So close I could almost touch him. He was seen at the Donville Masquerade."

Portia blinked as Ava pulled away and shivered. Clearly that location meant something to her friend. "I-I don't know what that is."

Ava sucked in a breath and looked at Portia with a flash of embarrassment. "Oh God, I sometimes forget you—"

Portia drew back when her friend cut herself off abruptly. "Forget that I what? What are you talking about? What is a Donville Masquerade?"

"You are an innocent and I think I shouldn't...I shouldn't have brought it up."

Portia's eyes went wide. Words like "innocent" certainly evoked a very interesting image of what this Donville Masquerade was about.

"You cannot leave it at that," Portia laughed. "Now that you have whetted my appetite with the implication that this masquerade has some kind of scandal associated with it."

Ava bit her lip and cast her glance to the side, and Portia caught both her hands. "Six months ago, you would have told me everything. Do not say that just because you are married and have...have...knowledge of more carnal subjects that you will lock me out."

Ava sighed. "Very well. But if what I tell you shocks you, I refuse to be blamed."

"What is it?" Portia insisted.

"The Donville Masquerade is held down in the hells the entire winter season," Ava began.

Portia shivered. Everyone knew about the hells, pits of ruination and despair where men...men like her father lost fortunes. Where women went to be ruined. It was dangerous and violent there, at least based upon everything she had ever heard.

"But why would they hold a party there? And why would your brother, a gentleman, have any part in it?" Portia asked.

Ava swallowed hard. "Again, I hesitate to share this with you. I'm certain your mother would not approve."

Portia pursed her lips. "At present, my mother thinks very little of me. She is too lost in her own...her own world."

Ava shook her head. "Oh darling, I'm sorry."

Portia ignored yet another painful topic. "You will not deter me by offering sympathies on that score. Tell me what this place is."

Ava sighed, but Portia sensed her ultimate surrender even before she said, "The Donville Masquerade is held in one of the notorious gambling houses down in the hells. According to my husband, they found that during the winter they would lose some of their clientele after a certain hour to the pleasures of a warm bed and a warmer mistress. Someone had the fine idea to bring the sin into the establishment itself. The masquerade is held several times a week and the debauchery is untamed."

Portia's eyebrows lifted. She was an innocent in body, of course, but she had once caught sight of a few very naughty drawings her brother had hidden away in his chamber. She had thought about them over and over at night while she touched herself.

"What do you mean untamed?" she whispered.

Ava shrugged. "Women displaying their bodies, men taking advantage of that, sometimes in the open between hands of cards."

Portia stood and clasped her hands before her chest. Her mind filled with shocking images, vague pictures of hands on skin, tongues and mouths and bodies rubbing together. They were things she didn't fully understand, but her body quivered at the thought.

"Ava!" she choked out.

"I told you I could not be responsible if you were shocked," Ava said, rising to place a steadying hand on her arm.

Portia shook her head to clear it. Apparently there was a great deal she did not understand about the secret world of sin and pleasure. "Is this *common*, to have...have *relations* out in public?"

Ava blushed so deeply that Portia had to wonder what exactly Ava had been keeping to herself about her relationship with Christian. Was it possible they...

Ava interrupted her thoughts. "Of course it isn't *common*, but there are places where men and women feel freer."

Portia swallowed. "Like the hells."

Ava nodded. "And because they have labeled their gathering a masquerade, the hidden and secret element makes those same places appear even safer to bare their bodies. But they are not safe at all. I have heard the hells and the masquerade can be quite dangerous, and who knows what mindset my brother is in currently?"

As Ava shuddered in fear, Portia pushed away her interest in the erotic elements of the masquerade. They were terribly inappropriate in the face of her friend's emotions.

"Oh, Ava," she whispered. "What can you do?"

Ava sighed. "As soon as the rumor reached us, I wanted to go there myself, but Christian is adamant. He refuses to allow it."

Portia's eyebrows lifted in surprise. This place must be terrible indeed, for Christian was normally indulgent to his wife. Even after their troubled past, it was evident he worshiped her, body and soul.

"He must have very good reasons to deny you," Portia whispered, thinking of Liam and beginning to fear, perhaps as deeply as his sister now did. "But could Christian not go himself?"

Ava's mouth tightened. "With my brother's deep and continuing hatred of him?"

Portia swallowed. There was a long history between the two men and their families. A history that had nearly destroyed her friend. And though Christian seemed willing to let the past go thanks to his love for Ava, Liam clung to it. No matter how deeply it hurt his sister or himself.

"I can see what you mean," Portia said. "Liam would not abide by that. But what about friends or spies?"

"Liam is too wary of everyone, but especially anyone associated with my husband. And he cut his own friends off long ago." Ava's voice wavered. "I am left feeling as though he is just outside my door, needing me, and yet I am unable to find the key."

Ava sighed deeply and sank back down into the settee. Portia took a place beside her and the two old friends linked hands in a silent display of affection and support. Certainly there was nothing *she* could do to help her friend and Portia felt as helpless as Ava did about it.

"I'm so sorry," Ava finally said after the silence had stretched for a few moments. "I have been nothing but selfish this entire afternoon between gushing and weeping. Tell me, how was *your* holiday? You and your mother traveled to your brother and his wife's country estate, didn't you?"

Portia flinched. If Ava had wished to find a happier topic, she had failed.

"Yes," she admitted softly, but said nothing more.

Ava leaned closer. "How was it?" she asked, but from her friend's concerned expression, Portia could see Ava had already guessed the answer.

"Dreadful," she admitted with a shake of her head. Images from the past few weeks bombarded her and she blinked to clear them from her mind. She could scarcely bear them.

"Oh, Portia." Ava sighed deeply. "I had hoped that your brother's invitation signaled a softening in his tone toward you."

"I don't worry about myself, his coldness is nothing new," Portia said. "But Hammond's cruelty to our mother..." She swallowed back tears. "She is still reeling from it. It may take her weeks to return to a more normal state."

Though she'd hardly call anything her mother did "normal".

"I wish there was something I could do, some kind of respite I could offer you."

Portia shook her head. "You know my brother wouldn't allow anything we might concoct. He guards his control over my mother too jealously and I wouldn't dare leave her alone for any length of time for fear of what he might do without my protection over her."

"But you deserve a reprieve from your troubles. Some fun." Ava winked. "Perhaps something wicked in your life."

Portia wondered again about the Donville Masquerade, but pushed the thoughts away. "There is no room in my life for such things."

Her friend's face fell at the finality of Portia's statement and tone. Ava squeezed her hand. "Anything can happen, Portia. Don't forget that and never give up."

Portia smiled as she extracted her hand from Ava's and freshened her tea. Ava might have faith in the power of the future, but Portia had long ago given up on what might be. She knew what was and despite anything Ava might say, *that* would never change.

"What about Lady Jane, the daughter of the Duke of Breadworth?"

Miles, the Marquis of Weatherfield, forced a smile for his younger sister. "She only just came out, didn't she?" he asked with a shake of his head.

Tennille hesitated long enough that he knew he was correct.

"How old is she?" he pressed.

"She is eighteen." When he arched a brow, she shrugged. "In four months."

"For God's sake, Tennille, that would make her fourteen years my junior."

His sister pursed her lips, but her eyes were filled with light and a touch of laughter. "Oh yes, brother, for that would be unheard of in our circles. A man marrying a woman so much his junior. The horror."

He couldn't help but laugh at her tone. "Yes, yes, of course it is common. But I could not picture myself marrying someone so young. What would we discuss?"

Tennille sighed and looked down in her lap briefly. "Then what about the widow of Lord Oakdoon?"

"She has four children." He moved closer. "Are you reading from a *list?*"

His sister flushed and pushed her hands beneath the table. Miles jumped to his feet and darted his hand beneath to snatch a paper from her fingers.

"You *are* reading from a list!" he said with a laughing shake of his head as he unfolded it. "You made a list of women I could marry?"

"I make lists of everything!" she said, trying in vain to snatch the letter as he lifted it over his head and read it.

"Great God, Tennille," he said, staring at her as he lowered the paper. "You have Lady Hippleton on here. Her husband died a week ago."

Tennille shrugged. "I need to keep it updated. You couldn't approach her with an intention for months, of course, but in time—"

He handed the paper back. "I'm not approaching anyone with 'an intention'."

Tennille pushed it away and sighed. "Miles, you are over thirty. You have been Marquis for fourteen years. I understand due to our...*past*...you wished to be free. But when will it be time to settle down?"

Miles' smile fell slowly. He and Tennille rarely spoke of the past. It was a dark place they had both departed years ago. He didn't wish to revisit it; he had always assumed she felt the same way. Now he saw brief pain flickering in her eyes and he hated seeing it. He hated the power the past, their father, still held over her.

"My dearest sister," he said slowly, picking every word and emotion carefully. "I appreciate your love and care more than you shall ever know. But I will choose a wife in my own time and way."

"Will you?" Tennille whispered.

He flinched at the concern on her face. "Yes. I assure you, I will. Someday."

"Someday." She smiled sadly. "Very well. I will leave you be, for now, because I see you wish to run screaming from my parlor."

"Not at all." He leaned forward to press a kiss to her cheek. "But I do have to depart. I have another appointment."

She nodded. "Yes, I'm sure. Will we speak again soon?"

"I will be back here tomorrow for Lydia's birthday party."

His sister's face lit up at the mention of her young daughter. "Good. She will be very pleased to see you. You are her current favorite."

That made any hardness or sadness in Miles' heart fade. "I feel the same way about her. I will see you tomorrow."

He squeezed her hand and then left the parlor. His horse was brought around in moments and he swung into his saddle. Of course he had been lying to Tennille. He had no appointment, he only wanted to escape her questions, her lists, her reminders of things he would rather forget.

He rode from the drive and turned onto the street. Turned toward the hells. The Donville Masquerade was being held tonight. It was a predictable gathering, but when predictability included wild sex and unfettered sin, that was perfectly acceptable to him.

Chapter Two

Miles adjusted his plain black mask and looked about the big, open room. Around him was a seething den of sin and excess.

Since its opening a decade ago, the hall had always been an infamous haven for gambling. There were tables spread all over the room, able to hold up to ten men at a time for various card and dice games. But unlike some of the more casual, friendly halls in the better parts of London, this place was filled with tension. Men who hadn't slept or shaved for days were scattered all around. One man sobbed at a table not ten feet from Miles, probably over the loss of what seemed to be a considerable fortune.

It was not an uncommon sight in this place. Miles had even heard rumors of underhanded bets over the virtue of daughters and the trading of wives. And if there was any hall to make such dangerous bargains, this was it. Sometime in the past few years, the proprietor of this den of depravity, a mysterious man named Marcus Rivers, had opened up his establishment to *other* activities.

Women had been allowed in. Mistresses, whores, even the occasional highbred and bored lady who hid behind a mask and offered herself for pleasure to the gamblers.

Some were discreet in their couplings, taking advantage of screened areas, private rooms and balconies. Others didn't seem to care where they fucked. Miles watched as a couple staggered drunkenly against the far wall, kissing with reckless abandon. The woman's moan echoed even in the din of the room as the man hiked up her skirt. She was bare beneath except for red stockings with a lacy garter.

She spread her legs, opening her body. Something her companion took advantage of immediately. He began to finger her slit as he continued kissing her with sloppy passion that had no concern about who saw them in the act. After a moment, he positioned himself between her legs and thrust, rocking himself inside her waiting pussy. He had a fast, driving pace, and his partner arched and mewled loudly as he rutted with her.

A few of the men at a table nearby watched with interest and the whores made their way over, hoping to take advantage of any arousal the scene might create.

Miles' loins stirred with desire, but it was faint. Strange. He had always been a man of powerful passions, deep and abiding desires. But in the past few years, his need had shifted. He still enjoyed the company of women, but there was something...*empty* about his conquests now, both in his own reactions and in the way he viewed those around him.

He shook his head at his thoughts. Perhaps it was the conversation he'd had with Tennille that put him in this strange mood.

He moved farther into the room. He had come here intent on gambling, but he wasn't opposed to brief pleasure if a woman caught his eye.

He scanned the room for potential subjects, but again was simply bored with his choices. Women in plunging necklines, their breasts almost bare, panting over any man who gave them a side-glance. They were all so bored and jaded...a bit like he was. There was no one to—

He cut the thought off as the crowd across the room parted and revealed a woman standing along the wall by herself. She had pale blond hair done up in a simple chignon at the base of her long, creamy neck.

Her mask covered half her face, but it was not of the ornate variety that the others wore as calling cards. It was blue and very plain, possibly handcrafted out of leftover silk from a gown. It didn't match her dress, which was a deep green and cut in a modest style that had little frills. Still, the fabric was high quality. He was left confused.

Was this a highbred lady or a lower-class one?

He moved closer, inexplicably drawn to her. She hugged the wall with her body, exactly like a wallflower at a ball at Almack's would do. She stared out at the room, her eyelashes fluttering as she blinked and blinked...almost in innocence, shock.

But was that real or affected? There were plenty of women who came here and pretended to be virtuous in order to play into the fantasies of certain men.

He had never been one of those, and yet he continued to move toward her. As he reached her, he realized she had dark brown eyes and they were dilated with high emotions that did not seem artificial.

"Hello," he said softly.

She jerked with surprise, for her attention had been so focused on the activity around them that she had not even seen him advance on her. She looked at him, cheeks flushed and those brown eyes widened with surprise and, he thought, recognition.

"I—hello," she whispered, her voice husky.

He smiled, sly. "You seem surprised to see me approach you. Do we know each other, my lady?"

She swallowed and then shook her head. When she didn't say anything else, Miles moved a little closer.

"I don't think I've seen you here before."

She shook her head again, her eyes focused intently on his face.

He smiled at her refusal to speak. If this was a game to obtain his interest, it was well-played. Her silence gave her an air of mystery that he found fascinating, indeed.

"You said hello, so I know you are *capable* of speech," he said with a chuckle.

She shivered, almost as if the sound of his laughter had touched her in an unexpected way. She hesitated a moment, then she said in another low whisper, "I am, my lord."

He arched a brow. Did she assume he was titled or *know*? He still couldn't tell.

"I'm sorry if you find me reluctant to speak," she continued. "I-I really don't know what to say to you."

He stared at her. "Your honesty is refreshing in this situation. I am a gentleman, so I would never do anything to make you uncomfortable. Would you prefer it if I choose the topic of our discourse? You may nod or shake your head in answer to me if that is more amenable to you."

She pulled the corner of her lip between her teeth and his gut clenched with a sudden desire. Her lips were full and he longed to feel them pressed to his flesh. Anywhere. Everywhere.

"Well?" he asked, trying to keep his raging desire from being too obvious. Desperation was never an attractive trait.

She nodded, a bit slowly.

"Good. I would like to know more about you—"

Before he could ask more, she shook her head hard, her eyes going wide and wild. He frowned.

"Nothing to identify you," he reassured her. "You say I have not seen you here before—have you *been* here before?"

She seemed to consider the answer. To consider running away, but then she slowly shook her head in the negative.

"I see." He looked her up and down. "Is there a reason you came here?"

She dropped her chin, breaking their gaze and leaving him feeling strangely...lost. She nodded.

"Hmm, that is very interesting," he said, stroking his chin. He thought of all the possibilities of why a woman...perhaps a lady...would come to this desperate and debauched place.

"Did you come to gamble?"

She immediately shook her head.

"Not to gamble. Then that must mean you came for the...*other* diversions this place offers." He couldn't help but grin, for that had been his hope with every step toward her.

But to his surprise, she took a side-glance at some of the couples engaging in public sensuality. There were moans in the air, flashes of flesh. Her breath caught and she blushed, but he sensed her deep arousal beneath her shock. So she liked to watch...well, so did he.

She shook her head, though it was much slower and less certain than the other times she had indicated the negative.

"Then did you come looking for someone?"

She nodded, lifting her face back toward his, her desire faded in an instant.

"Your father?" he asked.

She shook her head.

"Your brother?" Another hesitation and the negative, indicated by the shake of her head. He took a deep breath. "Your husband?"

Her cheeks filled with heated color as she shook her head.

"Ah, I see. Someone you care for, though." He tilted his head to watch her more carefully. This answer meant something to him, though he had no idea why.

Her response was slow, but she nodded once. He scowled despite himself. So the woman had a lover...or a love she was seeking. It could not possibly matter to him. He had no ties to her.

And yet he felt irritated. Frustrated. As if something had been stolen from him.

"Do I know him?" he asked.

She nodded swiftly and his body clenched. "I thought you said you did not know me. How would you know I was acquainted with the gentleman you seek?"

Her lips parted and she took a step away. "I—" she gasped, then lifted her hand to cover her mouth.

"Who are you?" he asked, covering the distance she had placed between them and then a little more, so that he crowded her closer to the wall behind her.

"Please," she whispered, and he narrowed his eyes.

Her voice—though she masked it by making her tone lower, huskier—bordered on the familiar, but he couldn't place her no matter how hard he tried.

"Who are you?" he repeated.

She moved, but he caught her elbow and drew her closer. She staggered against him, and the length of her body molded to his. He stared down into dark brown eyes, wide with fear, lips parted in surprise. She was warm in his arms and her shallow breath echoed in his ears and blocked out anything else in the busy room.

He should have asked her again who she was. Or slid a finger beneath her cheap mask and pulled it away from her face to reveal her identity then and there. He did neither. Instead, he lowered his face, covered her mouth with his and kissed her.

For a moment, she was stiff and shocked in his embrace. But then her mouth softened and she relaxed against him, surrendering to what he was taking.

He parted his mouth over her, darting his tongue to trace the crease of her full lips. They parted on a surprise gasp and he delved inside, tasting mint, a hint of sherry, the beginnings of desire as their molded bodies tangled.

Then, just as suddenly as she had offered a sample of surrender, she pulled back. He was too surprised by the abruptness of her departure to grasp her arm, and she slipped from his embrace, turned on her heel and bolted from the room and out the door into the street.

He watched the hem of her dress disappear into the night and felt like time had slowed. There was a pit low in his belly, something he recognized all too well, though he hadn't felt it for a long time.

He *wanted* this woman with a power that thrummed with his heartbeat and made his cock rock hard and achy. He would have her.

But first he had to find out who she was.

Portia could scarcely catch her breath as the carriage turned through the busy London streets toward her home.

"What was I thinking?" she moaned out loud, reliving every moment of the ill-advised trip to the Donville Masquerade with stunning clarity.

Why had she gone there?

To find Liam and help Ava was the answer she would have given if provoked beyond the place where she could deny the truth. And that *was* part of why she'd gone, of course. Ava was her best friend, Liam was...well, he was someone she had long cared about. If she could help them, she would do anything in the world to do it.

But there was more to her reasoning than that. Her conversation with Ava had stung her. Ava spoke of her having fun, being wicked, and Portia knew that wasn't possible. And yet she had dressed, fashioned a sad little mask and found herself in her carriage riding to a part of London where she most decidedly did not belong.

What she had found there was even more than she had ever imagined. She had seen men and women groping each other, half-naked for the world to see. Passion and pleasure had been in every corner of the room, stealing the air, stealing her breath.

She had been told her entire life that such things were wrong, but *seeing* them...watching them as they made love so passionately and publicly...while their bodies merged with what was so obviously pleasure...well, she hadn't felt wrong. She had felt...achy and strange and a lot of other things she didn't completely understand even though they made her want to touch herself so desperately.

And then Miles had suddenly been there.

Miles, her brother's friend...*former* friend. A man she had known since she was a girl, even before she met Ava. A man who still occasionally tossed her the crumbs of a dance with him at a ball. Out of pity, she was certain.

But tonight it hadn't been pity in his eyes or his touch or his...his kiss when he was with her. God, he had kissed her in a most improper way.

She found her hands gliding down her dress and settling between her legs. She blushed, glancing out the uncovered carriage window. They were still a few minutes from her home, but could anyone see her? Perhaps, but it wasn't very likely.

And the idea of it made her body twitch as she rubbed the spot between her legs that always felt so good. Her mind flooded with images from that night. People rutting on tables and Miles standing beside her. A woman spread out while two men licked her intimately, and Miles pressing her into the wall.

She rubbed harder, racing toward release as fast as she could. The images in her mind spurred her on and she arched her hips as her body began to tremble with pleasure. She gasped, her inner walls flexing with tiny explosions. Panting, she settled back on the carriage seat and waited until her heartbeat had returned to normal before she sat up straight.

She felt better after her wicked exploration, but not satisfied. She wanted...*more*, though she had no idea what that meant, really.

With a frown, she glanced out the carriage window a second time to see that they were just pulling up to the drive of the tiny house her brother let for her and her mother. But while the house should have been dark at this late hour, instead every light was on and there were two carriages already crowding the small drive.

"What on earth?" she whispered, reaching up to cover her face. To her horror, she felt the mask still on her skin, and she tore it off and shoved it in her reticule just as the carriage stopped.

Her driver helped her down with only a side-glance that told her he did not approve of her actions that night, but she hardly registered his expression. She was too busy staring at the seal on the carriage parked in front of hers.

Just as she feared in the pit of her stomach, it belonged to her brother.

"Hammond," she whispered, rushing up the stairs and through the door into the house. As it slammed shut behind her, she heard loud voices echoing through the small house. Male voices that melded with the voice of their single house servant, Mrs. Potts, and with the wails of Portia's mother.

Portia dropped her reticule and bolted up the stairs. Her mother's bedroom door was open and the cacophony of sound was coming from there.

"Mama!" she cried as she skidded down the hallway. She came to a stop in the doorway to her mother's chamber.

Her brother was there, as was Potts. Joining them was a man...a stranger, though that mattered little to her now. What did matter was that all three of them were holding her mother down on her small bed. Thomasina, Dowager Marchioness Cosslow, thrashed, screaming incoherently at all of them as she fought to get free of the imprisoning grasps of her captors.

"Stop!" Portia cried out as she jumped into the fray, grabbing the arm of the stranger without thinking and trying to tug him free. He glared at her over his shoulder but did not stop trying to control her mother.

Hammond helped him and, to Portia's horror, the two men tied her mother's wrists to the bedposts with thick coils of rough rope. Their mother continued to scream, though the sounds became less certain as she stared at each face around her. Portia saw the emptiness in her stare. The lack of recognition of any of them, of her surroundings, and her heart shattered with the pain of it.

When her mother was secure and could only tug at her binds weakly, Hammond straightened his jacket and spun on Portia.

He looked her up and down with an ugly sneer. "And just where have you been out so late?"

Portia caught her breath. She had never imagined her brother would be a visitor to her home when she slipped in during the night. But nonetheless she found a lie waiting on the tip of her tongue.

"I was invited to Ava and Christian's," she explained, knowing her friend would vouch for her no matter what, not that her brother would bother to ask. "I lost track of time. Why are *you* here, what is going on? Untie our mother at once!"

"I will do no such thing," her brother snapped.

"Your mother got out again, my lady," Potts said with a dark glare toward Hammond behind his back.

Portia's knees wobbled slightly as she cast a glance at her mother. Her thin lips continued to tremble, but her eyes were drooping.

"Did you *drug* her?" she asked, shoving past her brother to sit on the edge of her mother's bed. She stared into Thomasina's face. It was dirty, as were her bare feet, proving Potts's assertion that Portia's mother had been out.

"What other choice did we have?" Hammond barked. "Now leave her be and come with me. Mrs. Potts and Raysome will do the rest."

Portia glanced at the stranger again. *Raysome*, apparently. A big, burly man who was missing three teeth in the front. His skin was the color of oiled leather and his hands were huge. She shuddered.

"I won't leave her with that...that ogre," she whispered.

Raysome grinned like this was all amusing, but her brother didn't ask her again. Hammond grabbed her elbow and physically dragged her from the room and down the stairs to the sad little parlor near the front door.

Portia struggled the whole way, shouting out orders to Potts as she did so, but Hammond did not relent or release her until he flung her into a chair in the parlor and slammed the door behind him.

"We need to talk about this situation, Portia," her brother growled as he crossed to the sideboard and picked up a bottle that once would have contained whiskey. When he saw it was empty, he growled.

She shook her head at his glare. "What do you expect, Hammond? You do not give us enough funds to stock liquor in case you deign us worthy of a visit. Now what *situation* is it that we need to address in the middle of the night?"

He shook his head. "Mrs. Potts already told you. Mother escaped tonight."

Portia flinched. Yes, Potts had said that.

"Do not say escaped. It sounds as though we keep her prisoner here. We don't, despite your tying her like an animal."

"Perhaps she *should* be kept prisoner, either here or somewhere else," her brother muttered.

Portia tensed. Her brother's response to their mother's...problems...had always been to want to lock her away. To forget about her as if she had never existed.

"It won't happen again," she whispered, trying to keep her voice calm. "I promise you."

"You promise me the same thing every time she roams out into the street, raving and ranting and making a fool of me," he snapped, taking a step toward her.

Tears welled in Portia's eyes, but she blinked them away. "You have pushed us into this barely respectable neighborhood to hide us. I'm certain no one of any importance saw her."

"Out in her night rail, screaming at the top of her lungs as she headed for the park where there was a gathering?" Hammond asked, eyebrow arching. "I assure you, Portia, *everyone* saw her. How do you think *I* knew about it?"

Portia got to her feet and put her hands on her hips as anger overcame her. "I can only imagine how you knew it, brother. Spies, perhaps, that you make sure are watching us, not to render aid but to give *you* reasons to come here and torture me and torment her?"

He swung his hand before Portia had time to react, and the back of it hit her, hard enough that she staggered away from him as pain blasted through her face. She covered her burning cheek and stared at him, his face blank but his eyes filled with anger and upset and even guilt.

"You have one charge in life," he said, his soft tone belying the fact he had just struck her for the first time since they were children. "And *that* is to watch her. Your usefulness is limited beyond that since you are incapable of making a match that could financially assist this family. If you cannot take care of our mother, I will."

Portia swallowed, thinking of the burly, coarse man who had held her mother down when she entered the room. If that was how Hammond intended to take care of things...

She gasped out a sound of pain.

Her brother smoothed his jacket. "Will you attend Lord and Lady Steedmond's ball tomorrow night?"

Portia stared at him. "Are you in jest? After everything that has occurred tonight?"

Of course she meant more than this horrid encounter with her brother. She had been places, done things, her brother knew nothing about. She couldn't picture going to a ball as if life was normal.

He glared at her. "If you do not make an appearance, people will talk even more about Mama than they already do. You *will* be there, sister. Is that clear?"

Portia's mouth felt dry as a desert and she swallowed hard before she croaked out. "Perfectly clear, Hammond."

"Then there is nothing else for us to discuss. Good night," he said softly, turning on his heel and leaving her alone in the parlor.

She waited until she had heard the click of the front door and the rumbling of the two departing carriages pulling away before she exited the room. At the front door, she turned the lock. Not that it would keep her brother away. If he wanted to get in, to take her mother, he had a key and too many other means.

Up the stairs, she trudged, all warm and wondrous reminiscences from her night at the masquerade a distant and dull memory as she walked down the hall to her mother's room. It felt like it took an age, but somehow she reached the chamber and stepped inside.

Her brother's lackey, Raysome, was long gone, and Potts sat with her mother. The housekeeper had defiantly untied the ropes that had bound the dowager marchioness to her bed, and her mother was pliant as a lamb now that whatever drugs she had been given had fully entered her system.

"Did they hurt her?" Portia whispered as she took a perch on the edge of her mother's bed.

Potts shook her head. "A little rope burn around her wrists, but nothing more than that. Fools."

"She got out?"

Potts blushed before she nodded. "While I was doing the tidying up after supper. I thought she was asleep, Lady Portia, or I would have kept a closer eye."

Portia smiled as she slowly shook her head. "It isn't your fault, Potts. I should have been here."

Potts stared at her a long moment. The kindly woman had been hired by her brother years ago after his wedding, when he unceremoniously dispatched his spinster sister and troubled mother from his perfect home. Over that time, their lone house servant had been nothing but a caring friend.

"What your mother really needs is a companion to be with her all the time," Potts said softly. "Someone who understands the nature of her problems and could gently help her."

Portia squeezed her eyes shut. "That would be a wonderful thing, I could not wish for more." She sighed. "But Hammond would never pay for such a person, even if he had the funds to do so."

Potts blinked a few times. "My lady, I would not say this unless I felt you should know."

Portia shook her head in confusion and concern. "Say what?"

"Tonight, when he first arrived, your brother spoke of how it would be better to have your mother housed at Townshend House."

For a moment, the world swam before Portia's eyes and she was glad to be seated on the bed, for it was certain she would have collapsed otherwise.

"Townshend House...the *madhouse*?" she whispered.

Potts nodded slowly. "He and that Raysome fellow were talking about it quite a bit. I think Raysome may have some connection to the place. He was explaining how much the weekly rate was to house her there and saying how your brother could simply tell everyone she died. That a lot of the rich did that with their mad relatives."

Portia heard a sob echo in the room and realized it had come from her own throat.

"I have heard stories of that place," she said, barely able to form words when she couldn't breathe. "Their treatment of the people, the—"

She stopped, for she couldn't go on. The images her words created were too much. She pushed to her feet and paced the room a moment, trying to regain her composure.

"I-I couldn't stop him," she murmured, looking at her mother, who was jerking in her restless sleep. She moved closer to brush a few pale curls from her mother's forehead. "Oh God, I couldn't save you."

She glanced up to see Potts staring at her with deep and abiding pity in her stare. The servant was kind enough to look away so she would see it no longer.

"Thank you for your help," she said, smoothing her gown and stepping away from the bed. She nodded swiftly to Potts. "And for the information about my brother's thoughts on the matter. I certainly have much to think about. I'll stay in the room with my mother tonight, but we won't need anything else."

Potts rose slowly and nodded. "Of course, my lady. Good night."

She left the room, but once she was gone Portia couldn't keep up the façade. She sank into a chair beside the fire and let the tears flow. There was nothing she could do to stop her brother from doing something terrible. Nothing she could do at all.

Chapter Three

Miles stepped into the stifling hall at Lord Steedmond's lavish London estate. Looking around him at the crowd of mamas, debutantes and widows, he barely resisted the urge to turn on his heel and immediately walk out again.

Winter gatherings in London were usually smaller due to the exodus of some of the elite to their country estates for the colder months, but the fires and the damp made them close-in, steamy affairs. Those hoping to get a jump on the Season's rush were often far more aggressive here, and he already saw three or four chaperones eyeing him from the middle of the room.

After he said hello to his host and hostess, Miles scanned the hall for an escape. Instead, his gaze found Lady Portia standing by the wall. The sister of a former friend, the Marquis Cosslow, Miles had always liked her well enough. She certainly had more sense than any current crop of debutantes put together.

Tonight her face was pale and her gaze faraway, as it often was at these kinds of gatherings. For some reason he felt compelled to approach her, though he had no idea why. He had seen her at dozens of events and done no more than nod in her direction.

The mother of twin daughters just out for their first Season began to move across the room toward him and Miles darted toward Portia without arguing with himself another moment. Talking to her would serve a purpose, at least for a little while.

He reached her side and put a broad smile on his face.

"Portia," he drawled.

She jumped and lifted her gaze to him, and his body clenched. Her eyes were so familiar.

"Lord Weatherfield," she said softly, fidgeting her hands before her. "I did not see you come in."

He shook his head as he stared at her. To compare her to a woman at the Donville Masquerade was ridiculous. Portia was a spinster who probably didn't even know such places existed. It was only her pale locks and brown eyes that put him to mind of his mysterious lady, nothing more.

"I only just arrived," he said, forcing himself to speak. "When I saw you across the room, I could not resist coming to greet you."

She jolted. "Why?" she snapped, her tone far sharper than he had expected.

He tilted his head. "Why?" he repeated.

She swallowed. "Wh-why would you not be able to resist me?"

He wrinkled his brow at her tone and expression. "Am I not welcome, Portia?"

Her lips parted ever so slightly and she stared up at him, eyes filled with warring emotions. There were also faint circles beneath those eyes. What kept her up at night?

"Of course, my lord," she said, dropping her chin. "You and I have always been...*friends* of a sort, haven't we?"

He nodded, still troubled by her expression and odd demeanor. "I would like to think we have been. We have certainly known each other a long while."

She nodded, silent and again, he was ripped back to thoughts of another lady who had merely nodded or shook her head in answer to his questions.

"Portia," he murmured.

She glanced up at him and he saw her try to put on a façade for him. "I assume you must be looking for my brother at any rate," she said, her tone suddenly falsely bright. "Hammond is here somewhere, though I have not seen him since we arrived an hour ago."

He saw her lip twitch ever so slightly.

"No, I—well you know Cosslow and I are not particularly close any longer," Miles said. "Portia, are you well?"

Her lips pursed briefly and then she shrugged. "Of course."

But he could see that even though she pretended, there was something troubling her. And for some reason, that knowledge bothered him.

"May I make a suggestion?" he said, moving a little closer.

He had never noticed before how interesting her appearance was. With her wide-set, deep brown eyes and angular face, her looks were not the rage. Certainly there was nothing flashy about her to draw attention to her especially. But there was no denying she could be described as lovely, especially in certain lights and angles.

She shifted away slightly. "A suggestion?"

He nodded. "I think you should do something entirely irresponsible. Something that is pure fun and only for you. No one will ever expect it, Portia."

She stared at him for a long moment, her face unreadable. He expected her to smile or laugh or even tell him to stop teasing her. But instead, she turned away.

"It must be very nice to have such an easy life, Miles," she said, her tone low and hard. "I envy you. Good night."

He stared, frozen in place by her unexpected accusation, as she walked away into the crowd. He moved to follow her, but there was a touch at his elbow and he turned to find one of those wretched mamas staring up at him.

"Lord Weatherfield, what a pleasure it is to see you! Surely you remember my daughter, Rebecca."

He didn't answer for a moment, still stuck in the reaction he unexpectedly had to Portia. Then he shook it off and forced himself to focus on the rather horse-faced heiress who had been presented to him.

"Ah yes, Lady Rebecca," he said, hoping his voice didn't sound like a groan. "What a...*pleasure* to see you and your lovely mother again."

Portia toed her slippers off and stretched her aching feet. Lord, how she hated a ball, especially one she'd been forced to attend under the watchful eye of her brother. It had been an entirely unpleasant evening.

Except for a few moments when Miles approached her.

Initially she had felt nothing more than abject terror at the idea he had realized she was the woman he had kissed at the masquerade, but quickly it had become clear his attention had nothing to do with that night. Why that fact caused her a twinge of disappointment, she could not rightly say.

"Foolish girl," she admonished herself as she slipped from her room and stood before her mother's door.

Potts had informed her that her mother had been quiet all night, still dull from the effects of whatever drugs she had been given by Hammond and his lackey.

She opened the door and stepped inside. Her mother was propped up on her pillows, reading a book. When the door opened, she glanced up and offered a weak smile for her daughter.

"Hello, darling," her mother said, setting the book aside. "How was your evening?"

Portia swallowed hard as she moved to sit in a chair beside her mother's bed. "It was much the same as any other," she lied. "I am more worried about how you feel."

Her mother's face paled slightly. Although she never remembered all the worst moments of her episodes, she often said she had flashes from those horrible times when she became wild.

"I-I am as well as I can be," her mother said, her voice soft and filled with regret and sorrow. "Potts tells me I ran away?"

Portia shook her head. "Potts shouldn't trouble you with such things. There was no harm done."

She looked at her mother's scratched wrists and tried not to think of Potts' words about the madhouse.

"Was your brother here?" her mother asked, voice filled with faint hope.

Portia pushed from the chair and paced to her mother's window. As she shoved the curtain aside, she flinched at the bars her brother had installed months ago.

"Yes," she said simply. "Hammond dropped me off after the ball."

"I meant last night when I—I was struggling?" her mother said.

Portia turned. Her mother's green eyes, the ones she had not inherited but always wished were her own, were focused very intently on her daughter. In her moments of lucidity, Lady Thomasina could be quite astute.

"Yes, he was here," she admitted. "As much good as he did."

Her mother sighed. "You are too hard on your brother, my love. He has struggled greatly since taking over as Marquis and

39

having to clean up the messes your father left behind with his gambling. He may seem harsh, but he does his best."

Portia lifted her hand to cover the cheek her brother had struck the night before and tried to picture him "doing his best" without cruelty.

"That may be," she admitted, the words bitter. There was no use telling her mother anything that might upset her. "I do my best, as well."

Her mother's eyes went wide. "Of course you do, my love." Thomasina reached for her, and Portia took her mother's hand without hesitation. "I know you give everything for me, for your friends, for everyone but yourself. I only wish there was a reward I could offer you. I only wish I could see you having fun, experiencing some joy in your life."

Portia thought, all too long, about Miles. About his kiss at that dratted hall she never should have gone to. And she thought of him tonight as well.

He had said the same thing to her just a few hours before, that she needed to do something just for herself. Even Ava had proclaimed she needed wickedness in her life.

It seemed everyone believed they knew better for her than she did for herself. And yet if any of them knew what she had done, where she had gone, what she had felt...they would have all been horrified.

But she still wanted to do it again. To have one more night where she was with people who didn't give a care for consequences. Where she could be a girl who didn't exist. Where she could pretend to have nothing to lose.

"Portia, where did you go?" her mother asked, laughter in her voice. "You are suddenly very far away."

Portia moved toward her and leaned down to kiss her smooth cheek.

"Not as far as it would seem, Mama." She smiled. "Go to sleep, for you look very tired. Perhaps tomorrow we will be able to go for a walk in the park. A little fresh air might do us both some good. Remind us where we belong in this world."

Her mother nodded. "I would like that. Good night, my darling. Sleep well."

Portia smiled as she left the room, but she had no intention of sleeping. Not for a very long while, at least.

She rang the bell for Potts and pulled a dress from her closet. When the housekeeper came to the door, she smiled.

"Potts, tell Copper to ready the carriage. I'm going out."

Potts gave her a strange look, but then nodded and slipped from the room, leaving Portia to prepare herself while she tried not to ponder the folly of her life and her choices.

As she swept into the Donville Masquerade an hour later, Portia felt the heat of the room sink into her skin, beneath her gown and into the very pit of her stomach. At least the images around her were not as shocking this time since she was more prepared for them. She took them all in as she stared around her.

A woman was laying on one of the tables to her left, her dress hiked up around her stomach, her legs splayed to reveal her most private areas, and a man was fingering her slit as she stared up into his face.

Against a wall, two women kissed passionately while a few men watched them. To her surprise, the men had released their naked members and were stroking them, something she had never seen or even imagined before. So that was what a man looked like naked. It was rather terrifying and titillating all at once to see that great thing hard and ready for rutting.

"This is a mistake," she whispered, turning toward the door. She was about to leave when out of the corner of her eye she caught a glimpse of someone she knew.

"Liam," she breathed, facing the direction she thought she saw him go. But he was gone, vanished into the crowd.

She bolted toward the direction she thought she saw him go in, rising to her tiptoes as she scanned the crowd for a man with a scarred face and injured arm. But it was to no avail. If he had been there at all, he had vanished like smoke on the wind.

She pursed her lips. Would she give up so easily?

Turning, she moved to one of the tables closest to her. Six men played cards there, their faces filled with angry concentration. None of them were wearing masks and she didn't recognize them, but she still disguised her voice with a husky tone as she said, "I'm sorry to disturb you, gentlemen, but I'm looking for someone."

One of the men threw down his cards in disgust before he looked up at her. "Wot?" he asked in a heavy accent.

"I-I'm looking for someone," she repeated, now uncertain in the face of this man's unexpected anger.

He looked her up and down, then shot his tablemates a brief, toothless grin.

"Are ya now, missy?" he asked as he pushed to his feet. He was so very tall and he smelled of cheap whisky and tobacco.

"Yes," she managed to squeak out. "A man na—"

"If yer lookin' for a man, I'm that," he snarled as he grabbed her arm in an iron fist and pulled her closer. "You may be the prettiest little lightskirt I've ever seen."

Portia's eyes went wide as she tugged against his grip to no avail. "I—no, sir, you misunderstand, I'm not a lightskirt. I truly am here simply looking for someone."

"Well, you found me," he grunted as he pulled her across the room toward what appeared to be a line of alcoves hidden by screens. Already Portia could hear grunts and cries from behind them that were similar to those of the patrons who took their pleasure out in the open.

"No," she cried, tugging in earnest now, but her captor only laughed and squeezed her arm until it burned in pain.

"Stop!" she cried out, looking around for salvation, but in the midst of sin and seduction and ruination, no one seemed to be in any hurry to render aid. In fact, the few people who bothered to look up from their tables or lovers had a flash of interest in their eyes.

She was going to be accosted. Raped. In the backroom of a place where she did not belong. As the reality of that set in, Portia felt a scream bubbling up in her throat. But before she could express it, the man who was holding her was suddenly torn away from her with enough violence that she staggered as he released her.

She spun around to see what had freed her from his hands and was shocked to find Miles standing over the man, his breath heavy and his eyes flashing with anger.

"I believe the lady said no," he growled.

Portia expected the other man to jump to his feet and challenge Miles, but he only cowered there.

"She's a whore, Weatherfield. 'No' is a game," her captor whined.

Miles spun on her. "Was it a game?" he asked, anger in his tone that she wasn't certain was directed at her or the other man or both.

She shook her head. "N-no. It was no game."

Miles offered a hand to help her attacker up to his feet. As the man brushed himself off, Miles snarled. "Apologize."

He glared at her, but he muttered, "Sorry, miss."

Miles shook his head and shoved a bit of blunt into her attacker's hand. "Now go back to your *game.*"

The other man stared at the money and then eagerly returned to his table without a second glance for Portia or Miles. She stared at him, eyes wide, then turned her attention to Miles. He was glaring at her.

"You, come with me," he snapped, grabbing her arm much as the other man had done and taking her to the alcoves. He peeked behind a few screens before he managed to find one that wasn't occupied by moaning visitors.

Once they had some small privacy, he folded his arms and looked at her. "I don't know what your story is, miss," he began. "But it is evident you are far out of your element in this place. So why are you here?"

Portia swallowed hard. She couldn't say why, but she was reluctant to tell the truth to Miles, even though she knew he might be able to help her.

"I'm waiting for an answer," he pressed.

She masked her voice and whispered, "I was looking for the Earl of Windbury."

Miles' eyes went wide for a moment, not that she could blame him for the shock he expressed. After all, Liam had been in hiding for months. She doubted many people looked for him.

"I see," he said after a moment. His shock seemed to have been replaced by irritation. "I had heard, but—"

He shook his head and left the sentence hanging. Portia stepped closer. "What have you heard of him?"

He stared at her, his gaze burning hers. "He never keeps a mistress, you know," he said. "The best you will get is a few nights in his bed. If you are looking for a more permanent arrangement, I would be a far better choice."

Portia's lips parted. Was he offering to make her his *mistress*? This man who could have, and probably had had, any woman he wished? This man who had, at least in his mind, only seen her twice at a masquerade?

She shook her head. "I assure you, my lord, you don't want me."

Now it was his turn to move on her. The alcove was small and there was no place to hide as he slipped an arm around her back, gathering her closer, until her body molded to his. He was hard as steel against her softness and smelled of pine and mint and masculinity she couldn't define but made her shiver.

"You think I don't want you?" he whispered and his fresh breath stirred her cheek as he lowered his mouth to hers.

She lifted to meet him and realized she had been craving this kiss since the last time they were in this position. She had dreamed of it, dreamed of him. And even in the midst of all the upset currently in her life, Miles' touch was the one beacon of something *good*.

Even though she knew full well it could not last, that she could likely never visit this place again or see him unless it was someplace proper where he wouldn't recognize or desire her anymore. She knew all that and she didn't care. She wanted this stolen moment and she would do anything it took to have it last as long as possible.

If Miles sensed her desperation, that didn't seem to deter him. He delved his tongue deeply between her lips, dragging her closer until there was nothing between them. She wrapped her arms around his neck and let her tongue explore as she had been too nervous to do the last time he kissed her. She tasted him, uncertain of how to proceed, but enjoying how her body reacted as the heat between them rose.

He maneuvered her back as they continued to kiss, and suddenly she was being lowered on a narrow velvet seat in the corner of the tiny space. He knelt on the floor in front of her and continued to kiss her. His fingers slid along her cheek and stilled at the edge of her mask.

He slid one finger beneath the silk. She gasped and pulled away.

"No."

He frowned. "Why not?"

She shook her head. "Just let it be, Miles."

He hesitated, and then he returned his mouth to hers without touching her mask another time. She felt a flutter of something akin to disappointment, but shoved it away. If he knew who she was, it would only ruin everything. She instead focused on his touch and how her body reacted.

She...tingled. That was the best way to describe this unexpected feeling. It was as if every nerve in her body had come alive at once, making her skin sensitive to every touch and her stomach flutter like mad as he moved his mouth from her lips and down to her neck.

She shuddered as pleasure swept through her in a wave. He smiled against her skin and began to unbutton the back of her gown.

She tensed as his fingers moved adeptly. He was about to take her clothes off and then...well, then she wasn't entirely certain beyond what she'd seen here and through sketches, but suddenly she very badly wanted to know what he would do. And it wasn't as if seeing her naked would reveal who she was. He'd never know and whatever happened here would be a secret only she would keep.

Her dress drooped in the front and he met her gaze as he slowly lowered the cheap silk from her shoulders. Her chemise beneath had no frills or pretty embellishments, but it was almost sheer after multiple wearings.

She fought the urge to cover herself, only keeping her hands at her sides out of pure willpower. No man had ever seen her so exposed, and she could scarcely think out of embarrassment and confusion about her feelings.

Then he caught his breath and smiled, and all her thoughts cleared her fevered mind. If no man had ever seen her so revealed, certainly no man had ever looked at her like Miles looked at her now. As if she was...beautiful. Special. Desirable.

She wanted more of that feeling.

He leaned closer and she readied herself for another passionate kiss, but instead he pressed his lips to her collarbone. Then his mouth glided lower, lower until his mouth closed around her barely covered nipple.

She arched with a cry that she hadn't meant to voice but couldn't help. Not when electric, focused, concentrated heat was flowing from the place where he suckled and settling between her legs. An unexpected throbbing had begun that was quite like what she felt when she touched herself, only this was a more intense and powerful reaction.

He swirled his tongue around and around the peak, but despite the thin scrap of silk between them, she felt every touch with exquisite clarity.

"God," she whispered, driving her hands into his hair as she lifted her body to meet his mouth. She wanted more. She wanted to make sure this never ended. She wanted...

"Portia!"

Her eyes flew open, and she was met with bright light from the ballroom. A figure stood in the light, one who had pushed the barrier aside and intruded upon this private moment.

Her vision adjusted and she gasped as she lifted her hands to cover herself.

The intruder who had kept her from more pleasure, more passion, more utterly wicked exploits, was her brother.

Chapter Four

Miles recoiled as the Marquis Cosslow opened his mouth and one word came out, seeming to echo around them.

"Portia!"

He stared at the man, then slowly turned his attention to the lady in his arms. She was fighting to lift her dress, her cheeks hot red and her eyes sparkling with tears.

She did not deny the charge.

He slipped a finger beneath her cheap mask and pushed it aside before she could stop him a second time. His heart all but stopped at what he saw there.

It was all true. The woman he had been intent on seducing, the one he wanted in his bed so much that he could scarce think of anything else, the one he had offered to become protector of...was Portia. Portia, the spinster sister of a former friend.

Portia.

"Hammond," she said, pushing Miles away as she pulled the dress over herself and staggered to her feet. "What are you doing here?"

Cosslow glared at her with a coldness Miles never could have mustered for his own sister, no matter what she had done. He flinched at it.

"Your driver was kind enough to report to me about your whereabouts. I thought the man was drunk, and yet here you are splayed out like a whore." She dipped her head in shame, shame that Miles hated more than anything. But her mournful expression didn't put a stop to Cosslow's verbal attack. "The greater question would be why are *you* here?"

She glanced quickly at Miles, apology in her deep brown eyes. "I-I—"

She looked remarkably like a deer caught in the sights of a hunter's gun as she struggled for an explanation for the unexplainable.

"What the hell can you say?" Cosslow snapped and moved on her. He reached for her, but Miles caught his arm before he could touch her.

He rose to his feet and pushed Cosslow away. "Put your hand down, sir," he said, his voice deceptively quiet as the two men faced off.

Cosslow's eyes narrowed. "Fuck you, Weatherfield, I will handle my sister as I choose."

He was all but shouting, and his voice carried into the main ballroom. Worse, thanks to Cosslow's loud interruption, a small crowd was beginning to gather behind him, peeking in to see the source of the commotion. Some in that crowd were from a far different class than they and could cause no damage to Portia.

But many were lords of houses who would talk. Who would tell. Who would take such pleasure in destroying Portia's reputation.

"Mind your tone," Miles growled, motioning to the crowd.

Cosslow tossed a glance over his shoulder. "You two did this, not I. If you suffer, that is what you deserve. And you are lucky I do not raise my hand to *you*, Weatherfield."

Miles moved toward him. He was taller than Cosslow by more than five inches, and he towered over him. "Do you wish to challenge me? With fists or pistols?"

Cosslow, who had always been a cowardly bastard, hesitated, just as Miles knew he would.

"N-now see here," he stammered. "I have a right to be angry about my sister. I have a right to take her with me and punish her as I see fit."

"Like bloody hell," Miles snapped, ready to duel right there if it came to it.

There was a gentle touch on his arm, and Miles looked down to see Portia, her face streaked with humiliated tears, staring up at him.

"Miles, please. Please. I'll go with him. Don't make any more trouble for yourself, not over me," she whispered. With a start, she pulled her hand back when she realized it still rested on his forearm.

"Unlike the trouble you've created for *yourself?*" her brother snapped, an ugly laugh bubbling from his lips. "You stupid, stupid bitch, there is *nothing* you can do to fix this."

Miles stared at him for a moment, then let his gaze drift to her. He had always been a man of passions. Honor was secondary to him. But he was raised a gentleman. He certainly didn't want to turn into his father and become less than that.

And a gentleman only had one way out of this situation.

"The obvious solution to this problem is marriage," he said, the words echoing hollow in the now-silent room around them.

Silent until the crowd gasped.

"Marriage?" Portia repeated, the blood draining from her face. "Who would marry?"

"You," her brother barked. His tone was still cruel, but Miles saw the light of pleasure in his eyes at the suggestion.

"Who would I marry?" Portia said after a hesitation that seemed to stretch out forever.

Miles stared at her. She had come here to find a man, but it hadn't been him. She had said she was looking for the Earl of Windbury. Liam. His reaction to that was not one he wished to consider overly long, because it was entirely unpleasant.

"To me," he responded. "You will marry me."

Portia flinched as the carriage rumbled over a rut in the road and forced her to bump against her brother. He recoiled as if touching her would pass some horrible disease to him. Her heart ached at how low his regard for her had sunk.

But even more, she wondered about the regard the other man in the carriage had for her. She looked across at Miles. It was *his* carriage. A very fine carriage, much finer than hers or her brother's.

"This wasn't necessary," she whispered, her voice barely carrying, even in the silence.

"I would not send you alone with him in his current state," Miles said, just as quietly.

He did not look at her. He did not look at Hammond. His expression was utterly unreadable.

Hammond shook his head, lips pursed with disgust, but very intelligently said nothing. Portia was too humiliated to speak further, and the rest of the trip back to her small home was uncomfortably silent.

As the carriage stopped, Miles stepped from the vehicle before his driver could come to help them. To her surprise, he turned and held out a hand to her.

She bit her lip before she took his offering. Even through two pairs of gloves, she felt how warm he was. The warmth was comforting, despite the terrible circumstances that had brought them to this moment.

After she was safely on the ground, Miles released her and turned toward her home. She tensed. He was coming in? Her brother stepped down behind her and followed them to the door. Apparently, *everyone* was coming in. How she hoped Potts still had a fire going in the parlor or else it was going to be a very cold conversation, indeed.

Potts opened the door and her eyes went wide when she saw it was a party to greet her.

"Good evening, Lady Portia, gentlemen," she said, looking toward Portia with questions crinkling her eyes.

"Potts, I hope you can tell me there's a fire," Portia whispered, motioning her head toward the parlor.

Potts shook her head slightly, and Portia blushed. They didn't light fires in rooms they weren't using in order to save funds in whatever way they could.

She turned toward the men, determined not to show how bothersome this fact was. "We could light a fire or—"

Miles moved toward the room. "I only require a lamp, Portia. We won't be here long," he said over his shoulder as he entered her parlor without asking for additional leave.

She left her brother's side and followed Miles, watching from the doorway as he lit the lamp himself. He stepped back and looked around. What he saw could not be denied. Her parlor was a pathetic sight, with its worn carpet, lack of decoration and austere furnishings. He sent a brief glance her way, but it was unreadable. Still, her cheeks burned. There was a reason she kept no company.

"When will you marry?" Hammond asked from the doorway, without even closing the door. Anyone could hear this humiliation. His tone was almost bored with all this.

Portia shot him a look, but he didn't acknowledge it or her. He was...smiling.

Miles folded his arms. "Soon. There were too many people there from our sphere tonight. Normally they keep quiet about these things, but this is too good a piece of gossip and I'm sure the news has already begun to spread like wildfire. They will talk tomorrow. Tonight. Forever."

Portia sucked in a breath. She had expected a great many things from her life. First she had foolishly hoped for love, but when it became clear that was not going to happen, she had wished for a staid marriage and family. Eventually she had resigned herself to spinsterhood.

But never had she thought she would be the topic of utter and complete ruination. Or become half of a marriage forced upon a man she had once thought of as a friend.

She looked at him, willing him to look back. Willing him to smile. Willing him to forgive her for her part in this.

"Please," she whispered.

Miles' shoulders stiffened, but he didn't look at her.

"Shut up," Hammond growled. "Your choices are over now."

Portia squeezed her eyes shut. As if she had ever had any choices.

Miles jerked his face toward Hammond and in the dim lamplight she saw a dangerous expression on his face. Hammond was too stupid to notice it, but her brother was treading on very thin ice. She feared what would happen if it broke.

"We will discuss all of this further tomorrow," Miles growled. "I will come here at two o'clock to finalize the terms."

Hammond nodded. "I will be here."

Miles stepped toward him. "You will leave now, Cosslow. You will not come back tonight. Do you understand?"

Portia stared at him. Miles was defending her. Still. Even though she had caused his life to implode around him.

Hammond's jaw set, but he nodded once. "Fine. I have nothing to say to *her* at present anyway."

Her brother spun on his heel and moved toward the front door, where Potts still stood, gape-mouthed, since with the door open she had obviously heard everything.

Miles finally let his gaze settle on Portia. He held it for a long moment, long enough that she shifted beneath the focused attention he gave her.

"I will be back to speak to you, Portia," Miles said softly.

She met his gaze. She owed him that audience, that opportunity to have his say, but she feared it. His eyes were unfathomably dark and filled with depths of emotion she couldn't fully understand.

"I know," she finally whispered. "Miles?"

He stiffened and nodded.

"I'm sorry," she whispered.

He did not acknowledge the statement, but moved into the foyer and followed her brother out the door where they parted ways at their carriages. She moved to stand beside Potts and watched as the vehicles pulled away. It was only when they were gone that she turned to face her servant.

"Married?" Potts asked, her face pale.

Portia rubbed a hand over her face, wishing she could will away the pounding throb of a headache that had begun to overwhelm her. But perhaps she deserved such pain after what she done...caused tonight.

"Yes," she whispered. "Apparently I am to marry Lord Miles Weatherfield."

Once the words had been said out loud, her knees went weak and she gripped the doorjamb to remain upright.

This was real. It was not a dream. Her entire life had just changed with one foolish decision.

The note said she was expected at her brother's home before nine in the morning, so there she stood, in his parlor at eight forty-five, still exhausted from her late night and uncertain how to tell her mother that she was, apparently, getting married.

The door opened and she rose, but it wasn't Hammond who came in but his wife, Iris. They had wed two years before in a ceremony their mother had not been invited to attend. Since then, Iris had made no attempt to create a relationship with her husband's family beyond when they were forced to include Portia and her mother in events like Christmas this year.

Iris was not Portia's favorite person.

She pressed her lips together and forced civility. "Good morning."

Iris sniffed. "Yes, hello, Portia. Hammond will be down in a moment." Her sister-in-law folded her arms. "I hear you are *finally* to wed."

Portia swallowed hard. It was one thing to try to come to some kind of internal acceptance of that fact. Another to have her sister-in-law rubbing it in her face with a little smirk that said "the only way you can have a man is to force him".

"The details are not yet set," Portia said with a dismissive wave of her hand.

"Hammond tells me it is the Marquis Weatherfield who you've snared," Iris pressed. When Portia remained silent, she shrugged. "Well, he has a great deal of money, so that will help us all. And you two will owe us after this scandal."

"Iris."

Both women turned toward the parlor door. Hammond stood there, eyes narrowed at Portia.

His wife stood and gave Portia a little sneer. "Good day."

Portia nodded her head as Iris left the room, but her heart sank when Hammond shut the door behind her. She got to her feet and took a long step away from him. He watched her do so with a frown.

"I'm sorry I struck you, Portia," he said softly. "It was wrong of me."

She drew back in surprise. Hammond apologizing? That hadn't happened in years. Though he had never raised a hand to her in all that time either, so she supposed that could be the reason. She would prefer that option to the other, which was that he only took a kindly tone with her because of Iris's implication that she now could control the money her soon-to-be husband possessed.

"And now you will marry," he said, again with that false smile and those bright eyes.

She frowned. "You act as though I was courted. I do not think this outcome is a positive thing, Hammond."

He glared at her, as if pointing out the circumstances was uncouth. "Your methods certainly were not. That you would go *there*—"

"You were there," she said softly.

He shot her a look. "Only to find you."

She tilted her head. "So it is the first time you were an attendee of the Donville Masquerade?"

The way he jolted ever so slightly told her the answer.

"We are not discussing my vices, we are talking about your failures. And actually, I wish to talk about something else entirely."

Her brow wrinkled. "You do?"

"Mother." He spat the word like it was a curse. "We will now need to manage her differently."

"What do you mean?" Portia asked, her heart beginning to race.

He smiled very slightly. "With your marriage, you will no longer live with her, so she will have no one to look after her regularly. You recall Mr. Raysome from the other night?"

"The one who runs the madhouse?" When Hammond looked at her in surprise, she nodded. "Yes, I know who he is. You cannot mean to send her there! I have heard stories about that horrible place."

Hammond's eyes darted away from hers at that accusation. "Well, what other choice will I have, sister? Do you think Miles will take her in? A madwoman who humiliates her family on a regular basis?"

"She is far more than that!" Portia protested.

Her brother ignored her interruption. "Especially after you have already trapped the man into wedding you."

That stopped her. Miles wouldn't even look at her the night before. He had to despise her.

"You are lucky, in truth, that he will even take you," Hammond finished with a shake of his head.

She stared at him. "Why do you hate me? Hate her?"

For a moment, her brother held perfectly still, as if he was trying to manage his reaction. But she saw tiny cracks that showed anger, despair, that showed her how powerfully he felt about their situation, even if he covered it all up.

"You are lucky, Portia, not to have to deal with the consequences of our father's irresponsibility with money. With our mother's outbursts that are so public and so frequent. And with a sister who cannot seem to help by marrying a damn peer."

Portia's jaw tightened and she shoved to her feet. "If you think I have not suffered as many consequences as you have for all those facts, Hammond, you are a fool of the highest order. I'm going home. I think we have nothing else to say to each other that will not only make this situation worse."

He stared at her, apparently taken aback by her sudden ability to say no to him. He shrugged.

"Very well. I will join you there at two for our meeting with Weatherfield. Do try to keep Mother from ruining everything, will you?"

Portia fought a sudden urge to scream at her selfish brother and instead turned on her heel and went to her carriage. She felt a strange sense of satisfaction that she could walk away from Hammond with little consequence to herself now that she would not live under his rules or punishments any longer.

But the problem was that her mother still would. And she had no idea how to save her.

Chapter Five

"Great God, Miles!"

Miles flinched as his sister once again paced across the carpet in her parlor.

"Darling, won't you sit?" her husband, Viscount Richard Brinforth asked, watching her as closely as Miles did. "At this rate you shall wear a rut in the carpet."

Tennille shot her husband a dark glare, though Miles was certain there was a smile twitching at her lips. They had been married for five years now and had a child, so he was always taken aback when he saw the quick flashes that proved their enduring love for each other.

That was something he had convinced himself could not exist.

"What were you *thinking*?" his sister pressed, taking her seat as she had been asked.

Miles squeezed his eyes shut, and immediately images of the woman at the masquerade flooded his mind. Thoughts of the softness of her lips, the passion of her response and the horror of the realization that it had been Portia he had been seducing all along.

"I had no idea who she was," he said, his voice rough.

His sister's lips pursed and she sent a highly disapproving look in the direction of her husband. "I suppose that is meant to make me feel better?"

Richard lifted his eyebrows. "It certainly means you brother had no intention to ruin a lady, Tennille. You must give him that credit."

Miles smiled at his brother-in-law, grateful for anyone on his side.

Tennille sighed heavily. "I suppose that is true. But, oh, Miles. Forced into marriage by scandal!"

Miles shrugged. "You have railed on me so often about the choices I make in my life, I am surprised you haven't expected this outcome all along."

Tennille drew back at the bitterness in his tone. She softened her own considerably when she murmured, "My dearest brother, I know you. You are decent despite your every attempt at being a libertine. I *always* expect the best from you."

He frowned at her warmth and love. He appreciated it, but it did make this situation cut all the deeper.

"Then you must be highly disappointed," he said, lifting his hands in mock surrender.

"It could be worse," Richard offered, pouring Miles a sherry that made his sister huff out her breath in frustration. Her husband ignored her. "Lady Portia seems a nice-enough girl."

Miles arched a brow as he took the drink. "High praise indeed."

Tennille sank into a chair and shook her head. "You cannot judge Richard for his tepid compliments. She has left little impression beyond that. She keeps to herself and seems happy with her wallflower status."

Miles pursed his lips, thinking of how many times he had watched Portia sink against the wall, trying to make herself invisible. She had never seemed happy to him.

"She has her reasons," he said softly.

"Her mother, you mean," Tennille said with a slight shake of her head. "And the troubles her father had and brother seems intent on continuing?"

Miles felt anger rising in him as he recalled Cosslow's cruel words and demeanor toward Portia. He was furious with her, himself, but she had not deserved such censure.

"Yes," he managed to grind out past clenched teeth.

"What I wonder is why a lady of high breeding would be seen at such a scandalous place at all," Richard said with disbelief in every syllable. "It seems so outside of the quiet, reserved character she has always presented to the world."

Miles frowned. It *was* against Portia's character to go to the hells. But she had a reason, didn't she? A man she admitted she cared for. The Earl of Windbury, *Liam.*

His mouth was flooded by a sour taste and he shook his head. "I assure you, all these questions will be addressed by me." He glanced at the clock. "But for now I am meant to meet with Portia and her brother to finalize the terms of the marriage."

Tennille caught her breath as she got to her feet. "Oh, Miles."

He leaned over to press a kiss to her cheek. "I am sorry, my dear, for any shame I have caused you."

His sister's expression softened and she reached out to catch his hand. As she squeezed his fingers, she said, "When everything is arranged, bring Portia here for supper."

Miles stared at her. "Truly?"

"Of course!" Tennille laughed. "She is to be my sister, no matter the circumstances. Richard and I will welcome her with open arms into our family."

Miles looked at his brother-in-law, who was smiling and nodding in total agreement.

"Thank you," he said softly as he released Tennille's hand. "You are kind."

"We are family," Tennille said as she and Richard escorted him to their front door. "That means something."

But as Miles moved to his waiting horse, he couldn't help but think of how different the concept of family was to Portia. And wonder how things would change now that his hand had been forced and his future determined with one searing kiss.

When her carriage pulled into the drive after she had left her brother and their heated exchange, Portia tensed. There was a fine carriage already waiting there.

"Now what?" she muttered as she climbed down without the help of her Judas of a driver and strode toward the house. Quickly she recognized the seal on the side of the rig.

"Ava," she breathed, happy for the first time since the greatest nightmare of her life had begun the previous evening. She rushed inside, waving a hello to Potts before she burst into the sitting room.

Ava was perched on the edge of Portia's worn settee with a pot of tea before her and a few small cakes. Poor Potts, those were probably all they had for later in the day, but Portia didn't care about being hungry at the moment.

"I'm so glad to see you," she burst out as her friend got to her feet. The two women embraced and Portia only barely stopped herself from bursting into tears right there and then.

Finally they pulled apart and Ava motioned for Portia to join her on the settee.

"Tell me everything," her friend said without preamble.

Portia took a deep breath and then launched into her tale. Ava said nothing as she spoke, but leaned back. Her only reactions were the occasional lift of her eyebrows in surprise and tiny smiles at certain, very wicked interludes in Portia's tale.

Finally, Portia flopped back against the settee, almost as exhausted by the retelling as she was by the experience itself.

"You went there to find my brother, didn't you?" Ava said softly.

Portia turned her face. She had left out that part so that Ava wouldn't feel responsible for this strange turn her life had taken. Plus, she hadn't wanted Ava to guess the feelings she had long kept to herself. Feelings for Liam. Ones she had been so very willing to set aside in order to put herself in the arms of another man.

What kind of person was she?

"I'm afraid I did," she admitted, shaking away her troubling thoughts before Ava questioned her further about them. "After our conversation, I very much wanted to help you."

"Then I am sorry my troubles had a hand in the consequences you now face," Ava sighed. She lifted her gaze. "Did you—did you find—?"

Portia reached across and covered her friend's hand gently. "No. I thought I saw him last night, but he vanished into the crowd too quickly to confirm it. It may not have been him at all."

Her friend's face crumpled with disappointment. "Then it was all for naught."

"No, not all," Portia reassured her. "After all, I also went to that place and did what I did for—for other reasons."

"Which were?" her friend pressed, tone undecipherable.

Portia huffed out a breath for she was about to make a most shocking confession. Already heat flooded her cheeks.

"You kept telling me I deserved wickedness and my mother was talking about me having fun and even Miles said something to me at a ball about what I should and shouldn't do. I don't know. I thought I *could* do something wild and unpredictable. But I should have known I would be punished for such thoughts."

Ava let out a gasp. "Is that what you think this is? Punishment?"

"Indeed it is. The world is raining down a heap of pain for my sins, isn't it?"

Ava shook her head. "Is it so terrible? I thought you and Miles were friends as children."

"We *were*, though I am certain he now hates me. And why wouldn't he? I have stolen his future with my impulsive behavior." She shook her head. "And the talk...well, it must be very bad."

Ava shifted. "What makes you think that?"

"You were here without my calling you to me," Portia said with a shake of her head. "Which means you heard of my plight from some other source. Likely one that very much enjoyed sharing the details with you."

Ava swallowed hard and her pale face told Portia all she needed to know. "I won't tell you untruths. Yes, the word of your shocking appearance at the Donville Masquerade and your brother catching you in the arms of the Marquis Weatherfield are spreading like wildfire through our circles."

Portia covered her face. "Damn. Then I really have made an utter cock-up of everything, haven't I?"

"Perhaps not entirely. There are some who seem to hold you in high regard for catching a man after all these years," Ava said, trying to have a bright tone.

Portia rolled her eyes at her friend. "As if I went into the place looking to get caught this humiliating way?" She hesitated and her heart sank as a new terrible thought entered her mind. "Great God, you don't think *Miles* believes that, do you?"

Ava shrugged. "There is no telling what he believes. You should ask him, it is the most direct way of determining such things."

"I'm having a difficult time picturing that conversation," Portia sighed. In truth, she was having a difficult time picturing Miles in any scenario except for one where his mouth and hands were on her.

A wanton, she had surely become.

"What of your brother?" Ava said, shattering any pleasant wayward thoughts in Portia's mind.

She shook her head in surrender. "Hammond continues to despise me, though I believe he revels in the rich brother-in-law he will receive. I'm certain in his mind he has already gambled away whatever settlement they will come to. But even still he threatens punishment."

"What kind of punishment?" Ava asked.

She sighed. "My mother will be sent to a madhouse."

Ava's hand came up to cover her mouth as she made a little pained cry. "Oh no."

"Yes."

"He cannot mean it," Ava whispered.

Portia swallowed the harsh bile that had suddenly risen in her throat. "He does, I'm afraid. He had some bastard from Townshend House here a few nights ago to look at her and tell him prices. As if they were haggling over the disposal of a horse."

"What will you do?" her friend asked, tears flooding her eyes.

"I don't know. I suppose I must ask Miles for help now that I am under his jurisdiction. But he could hardly look at me, so I doubt I will find relief from him."

"You told me the two of you were quite...physically connected at the masquerade," Ava said after a long pause.

Portia blushed. "Yes."

"He wants you?" her friend pressed. When Portia hesitated, she laughed. "He wants you. You could...use that to your advantage."

"What do you mean?"

Ava shrugged. "Men like Weatherfield are driven by passions. An untouched lady who is willing to give him everything he desires is...well, I know of no man who would turn that down. If you feel he will resist helping you out of gentlemanly reasons, don't fear using your body to your advantage. It could be beneficial to you in more ways than one."

Portia stared at her friend in utter disbelief. "Barter for my mother's safety with...with my body?"

"From everything I've heard about Miles, I do not think it will be an unfair bargain to you. You liked what he did to you the other times, didn't you?"

Portia swallowed hard. She had spent a lifetime being told not to want physical pleasure, not to allow desire. And yet she felt it burn within her every time she thought of Miles.

"Yes," she admitted on the barest of whispers.

"Then why not take what you want *and* get what you need for your family?" Ava asked. "It seems as if everyone wins in that scenario."

"Ava!" Portia gasped, unable to grasp this concept that she would bribe her soon-to-be husband.

Before she could say anything more, there was a light rap on the parlor door. It opened to reveal Potts, whose lips were pursed together and pale.

"Lord Weatherfield is here, my lady."

Portia blinked in confusion, then turned to look at the clock. "I—it isn't two yet."

"Yes, but he is here regardless. And asking to see you."

"Demanding," came a correction in Miles' low voice out in the foyer.

Portia lifted her hand to cover her lips and stared at Ava. Her friend shrugged.

"Let him in," Ava suggested. "I doubt he would leave if you turned him away, and what good would it be to do so?"

Portia could hear her breath rattling in her ears over the whoosh of blood that made everything swim around her.

"Let him in," she whispered, hoping she would stay upright.

Potts gave her a long look, then nodded once before she pulled the door open more fully and said behind her, "Lady Portia will see you now."

Miles shook his head as he swept around her servant and into the room. "Yes, as if I couldn't hear everything. These walls are abominably thin."

Portia flinched. He didn't know the half of it. She could tell him horror stories of hearing the screaming fights of the couple who lived next door or having the brisk winter wind make sleeping impossible.

Instead, she stepped forward, hand outstretched. "My lord, what a surprise," she managed to say, her voice trembling on each word. "I did not expect you until two—did I misunderstand you?"

"No," he said, ignoring the hand she offered. "I came early because I wish to speak to you."

He looked past her to Ava. "Good afternoon, Lady Rothcastle. I suppose I should have assumed you would be here; you two are the closest of friends, are you not?"

Ava got to her feet and went to him with a smile. Portia flinched as he took the hand *she* offered without hesitation.

"We are, my lord. I understand congratulations are in order."

Miles blanched. "I suppose some would say that. Thank you."

Ava frowned slightly. "Portia is one of the best women I have ever had the pleasure to know, Lord Weatherfield. She deserves happiness and I hope, despite the inauspicious beginnings, that you will endeavor to grant her that."

Portia stepped toward the two as horror and shock mingled. "Ava! While I appreciate your kind words, Lord Weathefield does not need advice on how to treat me."

Ava arched a brow. "I hope not."

Miles pressed his lips together into a thin line. "Thank you, Lady Rothcastle. Now I hate to be rude, but I would like to speak to my...to my...to Portia alone for a moment, if you would excuse us."

Ava stared at him for a long moment, then she cast her gaze toward Portia. "Do you wish to be alone with him?"

Portia nodded. "Yes." She blushed. "I only mean Miles and I have a great deal to discuss and I would like to have a few moments before my brother arrives and takes over the proceedings in his usual highly unpleasant manner."

"Then I will go." Ava hugged her briefly. "Be careful," he friend whispered before she pulled back and smiled at Miles.

"Good day, my lord. I look forward to the friendship I'm certain we will all develop after your nuptials."

"Good day," he said, watching her go and quietly pull the door shut behind her, regardless of the propriety of them being left so utterly alone.

"Would you like tea?" Portia whispered, uncertain now that she was alone with this man who seemed to fill the room around her and steal all the air within.

"No." He stared at her, his dark eyes sweeping over her and giving no indication of what he thought. "Why were you there?"

Portia caught her breath at his abrupt question. "Wh-what?"

His lips thinned in irritation. "You heard me. Why were you at the Donville Masquerade, Portia?"

She swallowed. There was no way to explain what she did not fully understand herself.

"Because of your friend's brother. The Earl of Windbury? Liam?" he pressed, his tone suddenly cold. "You said that you were looking for him."

Portia hesitated and then nodded slowly. "I-I was."

Miles frowned. "Are you his lover?"

Portia staggered back from that stunning question. "How dare you?" she whispered, barely able to elevate her voice to a level that would carry.

He frowned, and she could see he took as little pleasure in these questions as she did. And yet he continued, unwavering.

"You pretend shock at such a suggestion, Portia, but you were very willing to fall into my arms."

She drew back. "Do you accuse me of having a lover or of being little better than a whore willing to give herself to any man?"

He shook his head. "I don't know what to accuse you of, my dear. You were in a place you did not belong and when I approached you, you offered none of the resistance I would have expected from a woman in your position. I have no idea why you would do what you did unless..."

He trailed off and stared at her.

She swallowed. "Unless?"

"Unless you were hoping for entrapment."

Entrapment. The word hung in the room between them like a slap and Portia took a moment to regain her composure before she responded.

"You believe I purposefully deceived you," she said. "With the intention of forcing a scandal."

He shrugged. "Your brother came very quickly to find us. And made a scene. I do not think it is beyond the realm of possibility."

Portia sighed. "You do not know the relationship my brother and I have, obviously. He would not help me cross a street, let alone plan something so elaborate as to entrap a man to wed. And as for my part in such a thing, Miles, you have known me for years. Do you truly think me capable of such deceit?"

"I think if a woman was desperate enough, she might be capable of anything," he retorted softly.

She flinched. Desperate. That was how people saw her. A *desperate*, sad spinster.

"I don't want this," she said, pushing each word out with enough clarity that they could not be misunderstood.

"Thank you," he said, hard.

She glared at him. "Is it what *you* want?"

He folded his arms, but before he could reply, the door flew open to bounce against the thin wall behind it and Hammond stepped inside.

"At least I do not find you two wrapped in some disgusting embrace," he barked as he glared at them. "But I do question why you are alone together."

Miles stepped in front of Portia and gave her brother as dark a look as Hammond had on his own face. "I arrived early, you ass, and was talking to your sister."

"What is there to talk about with her?" Hammond asked as he poured himself tea and ate one of Portia's few remaining cakes. "Your negotiations are with me."

"There are no negotiations," Miles snapped. "We will marry in a week. My people are already making the arrangements."

Portia took a long step toward him. "A-a week, Miles?"

He met her gaze and for the first time she saw a flash of softness there. Of kindness.

"It is the only way, Portia. The faster we do this, the sooner it will be out of the minds of those around us."

Her brother maneuvered between them and cut off her line of sight. "Very good, very acceptable," he gushed as he reached into his pocket and withdrew a paper. "Now, if you will just sign this paper that you have agreed to marry my sister, I would appreciate it."

Miles stared first at him, then at the sheet Hammond held out toward him. "You do not trust my word, even after all our years of acquaintance?"

Hammond shrugged. "I feel a need to protect my interests. And it also acknowledges you will receive no dowry in exchange for the marriage."

Miles glared at him, then snatched the paper and pen from his hands and scribbled his name across the document before he threw it back in her brother's face.

"There. Is that satisfactory?"

"Very much so. Please send all the information about the arrangements to my solicitor, as my wife and I will wish to attend, for appearance's sake."

Portia squeezed her eyes shut but managed to keep a sob from escaping her throat. It was done, finished, with as much romance as one might find in the slaughter of a chicken for supper.

"Now I would appreciate if you would depart with me," Hammond continued. "In case the neighbors are aware."

Miles clenched his fists as he turned to Portia. "I will speak with you more later."

She nodded but could manage no other words before she watched them leave the room and head to their respective carriages.

She was to be married. In a week. To a man who suspected that she had purposefully entrapped him into that position.

Potts entered the room to clear the tray of tea. "Are you well, Lady Portia?" she asked.

Portia turned to face her housekeeper and shook her head. "I thought being a mocked spinster was the worst thing in the world. I fear this ranks just above it in terms of humiliation. But it is done now, isn't it? And there is nothing that can change it."

Chapter Six

The last thing Portia had ever expected was an invitation to Miles' sister's home for luncheon the next day. And yet she sat in Lord and Lady Brinforth's beautifully appointed dining room the next afternoon with a spread on the table before her that she was certain the king himself would envy.

Miles sat a few places down the table from her, as quiet as he had been since her arrival half an hour before. He had hardly looked at her and she couldn't help the sick feeling in the pit of her stomach.

Was this to be her future? With a man who resented her and half-believed she purposefully entrapped him? Would he ignore her forever?

"Lady Portia," Lady Brinforth said as her servants finished serving the first course and slipped from the room. "Or may I simply call you Portia?"

Portia forced her attention to her hostess and smiled. "If you would like to do so, I would be happy to allow it."

"Good, then you must call me Tennille. I have always wanted a sister, I confess, and now my brother has finally provided me with one."

Portia shifted. Certainly Tennille must know how their engagement came about, but so far she had behaved as though their impending marriage was nothing but a pleasure to be celebrated. How she really felt, though, Portia couldn't help but wonder.

"We did hope your mother would join us today," Tennille continued with a quick glance toward her husband that spoke volumes and made Portia stiffen.

Her mother had been in a state for a few days. Portia hadn't even told her yet about the wedding.

"She is...not well, I'm afraid," she stammered, using the same terms she had been using for years to describe her mother's problems. "I'm sure she would have loved to join us were she able, but she rarely leaves the house."

Tennille's expression softened. "Well, if your mother will not be able to help you plan the wedding, perhaps I can be of assistance in her stead. You have begun having your dress made?"

Portia shot Miles a desperate look in the hopes she might find an ally. He still had his gaze firmly on his plate.

"With everything happening so quickly, I fear I hadn't thought of it," she explained, hoping she wouldn't have to add she had no funds for such things.

"But you must!" Tennille said with a laugh. "I will send my own seamstress to you immediately!"

Portia clutched her napkin. "You are too kind, but I couldn't put you out in any way."

Tennille seemed confused. "To share my seamstress's name with you? It does nothing to put me out at all. A pretty silk, perhaps in gray, would look lovely on you."

Portia caught her breath. How many times had she pictured a happy wedding? This was not it.

"You are so very kind, but I can't. I will...I will have to make due with something I have already."

Tennille stopped speaking and stared at her. In that horrible moment, Portia realized her future sister-in-law had realized the problem. Funds, or lack of them.

"It is something you and my brother will decide, I'm sure," she said after an awkward moment had passed.

"Yes," Miles finally said, joining the conversation at last with a brief glance for her. "Portia and I do have a great deal to discuss. I will escort you back to your home after our luncheon, Portia, and we can talk about the details of our wedding."

Portia nodded, but inside she wondered when they would discuss the details of their *marriage*. What did Miles expect from her? How would he treat her? Would he ever touch her again now that he knew who she was?

Or had his desire for her died the moment her mask was removed?

Miles looked across the carriage to Portia as they took the trip across London back to her tiny hovel of a home. She didn't seem to notice his regard as she stared out the carriage window with a faraway expression.

He wanted her.

It was a strange thing, to see the young woman he had known and spoken to and even pitied over the years and now feel a driving, powerful passion to possess her body. But he did. It kept him up at night. It made him ache with desire.

And yet he had not acted on that impulse since they were caught together at the masquerade. There were so many questions, so many plans to make, that he had been able to avoid his need.

Until now when he sat in a quiet vehicle with her with at least half an hour of privacy stretched out before them.

"Look at me," he whispered.

She glanced over to him in surprise. "Miles?"

The way she said his name undid him. He moved to her side of the carriage with aching slowness and took a deep breath of her scent. How he hadn't made the connection between his mystery woman and Portia, he couldn't be sure now. They both smelled of fresh lemon and lilac. He should have known.

Perhaps he did know, on some level. Perhaps that was why he had been so driven to say hello to her at that ball the night following their first heated encounter at the masquerade. Perhaps his body had been leading him to Portia all along.

He pressed his palm to the angle of her jawline and spread his fingers open. She gasped at the contact, but didn't pull away. She merely stared up at him, dark eyes wide, body shaking.

"Miles," she said again, her voice broken and filled with need he couldn't deny.

He tilted her face and kissed her. Immediately, he was struck with a feeling of coming home that was quickly replaced by a raging desire that boiled his blood and inspired fantasies of hiking her skirts and rutting with her here and now.

Somehow he controlled that and instead dove into the pleasures of her mouth. He stroked his tongue along hers, reveling in the tiny moan that escaped her lips into his mouth. He wrapped an arm around her back and drew her closer, closer.

She shuddered and her hands lifted to clutch at his lapels. He was utterly undone and he knew he could no longer control himself. He dragged his mouth to her throat, sucking at the slender column even as he began to inch her skirts up around her thighs. She gasped, and for a moment she tensed, but as he cupped her knee and began to glide his hand upward, she fell back against the carriage seat with a sigh of surrender that rocked him to his very core.

He would not take her. But he would have her in some way.

He found the slit in her flimsy drawers and parted it to press him palm flat against her sex. She was already wet and his cock swelled against the uncomfortable tightness of his trousers.

"Miles," she whispered as he ground his palm down against her body, creating pressure against just the right spot. Her breath caught, and she turned her face into his neck, shuddering as he increased the stroke of his hand. When she was trembling he slid a finger into her sheath and held back a low, possessive groan.

She was slick and hot and oh, so very tight around him. He pressed a thumb to her clitoris and began to circle the nub as he rocked his finger in and out, in and out. Her back arched and she gave a little squeal as her body began to convulse from release. He continued to stroke her through the crisis and only stopped when she went limp against the carriage seat.

He pressed another kiss to her parted lips before he glided her skirts back into place and moved to his original position in the carriage, just as the vehicle came to a stop at her doorstep.

She stared at him in disbelief. "I never imagined it could be so powerful."

He arched a brow at that unexpected observation and could not help wondering how much she knew about the pleasures of the flesh. But he did not ask as his footman opened the door and held it for their exit. Miles stepped from the carriage and held out a hand to her. The same hand that had touched her so intimately not a moment before. She stared at the outstretched fingers for too long before she took them and allowed his assistance.

Mrs. Potts opened the door and her face reflected surprise at Miles being there. "Good afternoon, my lady, my lord."

"Potts, isn't it?" Miles asked, handing over his greatcoat to the blinking housekeeper.

"Yes, sir."

"Excellent. Will you bring us tea in that little parlor? And then Lady Portia and I will require a bit of privacy." He looked at his apparent fiancée closely. "We have a great deal to discuss."

Portia trembled as Potts poured the tea and then stepped to the door. "Will you require anything further?"

"No," Miles answered for her. "Close the door."

Potts shot Portia a look but did as she was told. As the click of the door shutting all but echoed in the room, Portia shifted with discomfort.

"You should not be ordering my servants about."

He arched a brow. "That is what you are worried about in this moment?"

She stared at him. "What am I worried about in this moment could fill a room in itself, one far bigger than this one."

He motioned to the settee and took his own place on the chair. She tried not to think about what her twinge of disappointment meant, not when her body still tingled from his intimate touch in the carriage.

What he had done to her body was far more intense than any pleasure she had ever brought to herself.

"I think we have established that this marriage is not something either of us would have chosen. Certainly not in this matter that is thrust upon us?" Miles said.

Her warmer thoughts faded. "I thought you wished to accuse me of entrapping you."

He frowned, and the lingering doubt on his face made her turn her gaze from him. He didn't trust her, and she supposed she deserved it. But she had little choice but to trust *him.*

"Miles, I realize I don't deserve it, but I need your help," she whispered. She looked up and he was staring at her intently.

"My help?" he repeated. "With what?"

She drew in a breath. The idea of explaining the full horror of her life was so painful she could hardly take it. More to the point, she wasn't sure she could fully explain her plight.

"Will you come with me?" she asked, getting to her feet. "Please."

He hesitated, then motioned toward the door. "Lead the way."

As she exited, Potts poked her head out of the dining room. When she saw Portia going upstairs, she stumbled into the foyer. "Where are you going, miss?"

"Is my mother...is my mother dressed?" Portia whispered.

Potts recoiled. "Lady Portia..."

Portia sucked in a breath. "I know. I know it is a vile intrusion, but I need Miles to see. It is the only way to ensure her future."

Potts squeezed her eyes shut and Portia could see the housekeeper struggling. Miles remained silent through their exchange, only watching Portia carefully.

Finally, Potts nodded. "She is dressed. In her chamber."

Portia swallowed and started up the stairs again. "Showing you is the only way," she murmured, more to herself than to Miles.

And it was possibly the way she would send the man screaming away from her, despite the ruination that would follow for them both. But it was a risk she would have to take...for her mother.

She hesitated outside her mother's door, staring at the barrier that separated her from something she dreaded deeply. She turned.

"People speak of my mother and her...her outbursts, I know," she began with as much dignity as she could muster. "But no one knows the full extent of her pain. I want you to see, but Miles, I haven't told her yet about our engagement."

He stared at her in surprise. "You haven't?"

"No." She shifted.

"You must tell her at some point," he said with a shake of his head.

"It is complicated," she pleaded. "And I will tell her. I will."

Drawing a deep breath, she lightly knocked and turned the knob to let herself into her mother's room. As the light from the hall joined the low light from her mother's lamp, she heard Miles gasp.

And why wouldn't he? She tried to forget it when she came into this chamber, but she knew what he saw.

The room was sparsely furnished with only a chair and a bed, and the walls had padding on them. The windows had been barred and there was a crack in the glass from a time when her mother had thrown something at an intruder who did not exist. The cheap wallpaper was torn and hung in strips from where her mother had pawed at it.

Her mother sat on the lone chair, blond hair uncombed around her face. She was softly singing as she stared off into nothingness.

Portia swallowed at tears that choked her and stepped into the room. "Mama?"

Her mother did not respond, but continued her empty crooning beneath her breath.

"Mama," Portia repeated, setting her hand down on her mother's shoulder.

Her mother jolted and looked up at Portia with pure terror on her face. When a moment passed and she finally recognized her daughter, the high emotion faded, if only slightly.

"Hello, my dear," her mother said, almost sounding normal.

"Good afternoon, Mama. How are you feeling?" Portia asked with a false smile. She refused to look at Miles. Not now.

Her mother blinked. "I-I am well enough."

The hesitation made Portia's heart sink. There were sometimes voices in her mother's head. She wondered what they were saying now.

"Mama, we have a guest," she said softly.

Her mother jerked her face toward the door and stared at Miles. "Who is he? Another man from the madhouse like your brother sent?"

Portia finally looked at Miles herself. His face was so unreadable, she couldn't tell if he felt horror or pity or disgust or nothing at all.

"No, my lady," he finally said, moving closer slowly. "I am Miles. I was a friend of your son and daughter when they were young. I visited your old house where Hammond now lives while you were still in residence there."

Her mother wrinkled her brow, and Portia could see her trying to remember. But memories of that house brought her pain and she had developed the ability to cut them off. Portia watched her do just that as her face went blank again.

"I'm sorry. I don't recall."

Portia smiled. "It—it's all right, Mama. I have news. Miles and I are to be married."

Her mother paused for a moment as the words sunk in, then looked at Miles, then back to her. "Married?" she repeated on the barest of whispers.

Portia nodded. "Yes. And soon." She swallowed. "Before the week's end."

There was a very long silence. Long enough that Portia leaned toward her mother.

"Am I invited to the wedding?" her mother whispered.

Portia squeezed her eyes shut in pain. Her brother had excluded their mother from his wedding just as he almost always excluded them both from his life.

Portia looked at Miles. He moved forward another step.

"Of course you will be, my lady. No one would deprive you of seeing your only daughter wed."

Portia smiled at Miles through her tears as her mother's face relaxed. "Very good. I'm so pleased, Portia." She blinked a few times. "What about your father?"

Portia tensed. She hadn't realized her mother's dream world had come to include her father again. She hadn't mentioned him as though he still lived for a long time.

"Mama, you remember, don't you?" she whispered, pressing a hand to her mother's shoulder. "Papa is dead."

Her mother stiffened and stared up at her. "Dead."

"Yes, eight years ago. Do you remember?"

Her mother shuddered. "I don't know."

"Oh, Mama," Portia whispered as she leaned down to press a kiss to her forehead.

"Lady Portia?"

Portia turned to find Potts standing in the doorway. "I'll stay with her."

Portia nodded her thanks. "I'll come speak to you again in a little while, Mama. I have a few things to discuss with Miles."

Her mother blinked a few times again and then nodded. "Very well, dear."

She squeezed her mother's hand and then turned to Miles without meeting his eyes. "Shall we step out?"

He ignored her and instead bent to take her mother's hand. "Lady Cosslow, I shall look forward to seeing you at the wedding. Good day."

Her mother smiled and this time the expression was reminiscent of who she had been years ago. But as Miles led the way out of her mother's chamber and Portia shut the door, she heard her mother ask Potts, "Is Oliver truly dead, Potts?"

She leaned against the door as exhaustion overwhelmed her.

"There you have it, Miles," she said, trying to keep her focus on the wooden floor beneath her feet.

"Yes," he said, softly, gently. "Why don't you come back downstairs and we can discuss this more thoroughly?"

She nodded and followed him back to the dingy parlor. She made no offer to pour more tea, she simply sank into the settee and then looked at him.

"I hope you do not feel doubly lied to after seeing the state my mother has degenerated to."

He held her gaze. "I feel nothing but shock and sadness at the condition of your mother, Portia. It has been a long time since I was in your home, but I remember her far differently. How long has it been so dire?"

She hesitated. Her natural inclination was to play down her mother's woes. But she had to be honest with Miles.

She shivered. "It started when I was eight or nine, her episodes. But her problems progressed for years. I would say when my father died and my brother took over as Marquis that it truly hit a peak."

"So for eight years you have endured this," he murmured.

"No, my *brother* endures it. I simply grieve what should have been." She rubbed her eyes. "You know some of it, I'm certain. Her outbursts have occasionally been very public. It is why my brother hid us away in this hovel, though she escapes from time to time even today and roams the streets making what Hammond calls a spectacle." She frowned. "As if she could control it."

"I am sorry," Miles said, his tone gentle.

She shook her head. "Don't be sorry. Not when you could help me."

He took a small step away. "Yes, you asked for my help before we met with your mother. What is it you think I can do?"

Portia drew a breath. "My brother wants to have her committed to Townshend House. He has wished to do so for some time, but I believe he will follow through when I am no longer in this home to watch over our mother."

"He would put his own mother in such a place?" Miles breathed.

She nodded. "Both to rid himself of her and to punish me for humiliating him thanks to the circumstances of our engagement."

Miles' lips pressed hard together. "*This* is exactly why I am no longer friendly with him."

Portia drew back, uncertain what he meant by that comment. But at present she had more important matters to attend to.

"I cannot see her put in such a place, Miles. It would kill her. And it would break me."

He looked as though he intended to speak, but she rushed to keep him from denying her without hearing her out fully.

"I understand you likely do not want to claim responsibility for someone with her difficulties, but I would not ask you to do something without offering you something in return."

He hesitated. "Something in return?"

She nodded. Her cheeks felt hot and her hands shook as she continued, "Miles, there is something between us. A physical draw. And my understanding is that many wives of our sphere do not allow their husbands to take liberties beyond the barest requirement for producing a child."

His eyes went wide. "A-and?"

"Wh-whatever you wanted me to do...whenever you wanted me to do it...I would not argue. I would not disagree." She swallowed hard past a suddenly thick tongue. "Miles, I would give myself to you entirely."

Chapter Seven

Miles could hardly speak as he stared at Portia. She sat primly on the edge of the settee, for all the world a lady, but offered him the pleasures of her body in any and every wicked way he could imagine.

"Are you bargaining for the safety of your mother with your body?" he asked, knowing full well that was what she had done, but somehow needing to hear it again.

She shifted. "Yes. I realize it is small payment for what I ask, but I hope you would find it a worthwhile-enough temptation that you would say yes."

Miles turned away from her and paced to the window. What she must think of him to believe she had to offer herself in order to gain his assistance. He thought of Lady Cosslow in that horrible room, so lost to the world, and his heart ached for everything Portia had been through. He would no more see his future mother-in-law sent to a horrible place like Townshend House than he would see his own beloved sister placed there. That Hammond would even consider such a thing made his stomach turn.

He glanced at Portia. She was worrying her hands together in her lap as she awaited his decision. She had shattered in pleasure in the carriage. What else he could do to her...

And she had no idea that he would help her mother without asking for anything in return.

So why not take advantage of her...well, desperation when he was honest with himself. It wasn't gentlemanly, but it was oh, so very tempting, wasn't it?

He cleared his throat. "Do you know what you are offering me?"

She hesitated. "I have heard a little, looked at a few pictures and I have...I have touched myself sometimes in the dark of my bed."

He groaned as images of such a thing bombarded him. "I am a man of certain appetites, Portia. If you tell me I can do with you what I wish, I will take full advantage of that offer. I will do things to you, with you, that you have never dreamed of. Would you really be ready for that?"

Her eyes were wide and glassy as she nodded. "I keep my word. If I say I will do what you wish, I will. Even if it hurts."

"It won't hurt," he reassured her. "I will make sure of that. What you felt in the carriage, did that hurt?"

She shook her head. "No."

"That is only the beginning. I will make you feel so much better." He moved toward her and she gasped as he sank onto the settee next to her. "I will make you beg me for more. I will make you weak with pleasure. But I cannot promise that you won't fear what I want. That you won't be changed by it."

Her breath came heavy for a charged moment, and then she nodded. "If you help me, I will do anything you desire, Miles. Anything."

He drove his fingers into her silky blond hair and tilted her face toward his. His mouth collided with hers and he kissed her, pouring passion into her with his lips the same way he would soon with his fingers, his tongue, his cock. Oh, the ways he would debauch her.

He pulled back. "I take your offer, Portia. Your brother, greedy bastard that he is, will easily fold under my demands to remove your mother from his care."

"Are you sure?" Portia shook her head. "If he feels he can gain something from refusal, he will do it."

Miles scowled. "If he doesn't, I will make certain he changes his mind. You will not have to worry about your mother's future."

Portia went limp in his arms as she buried her face into his shoulder.

"Thank you," she murmured, and her voice cracked as she trembled in his arms. He stared down at her, smelling the freshness of her hair, feeling the warmth in her quivering limbs. Slowly, he wrapped his arms around her and held her. A powerful shot of protectiveness rocked him as he did so. Now that he had seen the full power of what she had endured, he wanted to help her. To make her smile. To give back a tiny bit of what circumstance and selfish men had taken from her.

Couldn't he do that? Couldn't he shower her with kindness and joy without entangling emotions? Since they were to be married either way, it seemed like he could give her that.

She pulled away and looked up at him with a shake of her head. "I'm sorry."

He stood and smoothed his jacket. "Don't trouble yourself, Portia. I wasn't offended by your emotion. I would be more offended if you were like your brother and felt nothing toward your mother. Now I have some arrangements to be made with him about this, since I fear he will act swiftly if I don't intercept him."

Portia got to her feet and followed him into the foyer. "Thank you."

He turned and looked her up and down in her cheap garment and her dim and ugly hall. "Portia, my sister's dressmaker will call tomorrow for you and for your mother."

"Oh no—" she began, cheeks flushing just as they had at his sister's earlier in the day.

"Hush. I will pay for it and I will brook no refusals," he said with a dismissive wave of his hand. "You are to be my wife, no matter what circumstances brought us to this. I will not see you treated as anything else from now on."

Portia nodded after another moment's hesitation. "Very well."

"Good day," he said as he exited the house. But as he walked to his horse, he smiled. Indeed, he had much to plan. Both for Portia's new life, and for the pleasures he would shower over her as soon as she was his, body and soul.

By the next morning, Portia had spent hours making a list. A list of everything she would have to do to ready for a wedding in a few days' time. It was very long and so overwhelming that she feared she might weep.

She rested her head on the edge of the flimsy dressing table in her chamber and sighed heavily. She was about to lift it again and return to her work when she heard the bell downstairs ringing to indicate a guest.

She paused and listened as Potts answered it and let someone inside, a woman judging by the lilting tones floating through the thin walls to Portia's room. She stood up and turned toward the door, ready when Potts knocked, then entered a moment later.

"There are two ladies to see you," Potts said softly, but there was a twitching to her lips that seemed to indicate pleasure. "A Miss King and Lord Weatherfield's sister, Lady Brinforth."

Portia's lips parted. "Have you already shown them the parlor?" she asked.

Potts nodded. "Where there is a roaring fire and a pot of tea, Lady Portia."

"Well, at least there is that," Portia sighed.

Potts smiled. "There will be more than that very soon. Lord Weatherfield sent a man here this morning to deliver a full larder of food, wood for the fires. He also told me there would be furniture arriving this afternoon for the parlor and our chambers."

Portia blinked, unsure if what she was hearing had been brought on by a sleep-deprived delusion. "I don't understand."

"It seems the man is intent on ensuring your comfort, my lady," Potts said with a wink. "Even if you will only live here a few days longer. Now I'll go down and tell the ladies you'll be joining them shortly."

Her servant turned and departed the room, leaving Portia blinking after her in continued shock. Miles didn't want to marry her, yet he did desire her and seemed to be driven to take care of her needs. What did it all mean?

She smoothed her gown and slipped downstairs. Outside the parlor, she took a deep breath. The women inside must judge her terribly on the current state of her home, but she had to keep her head high.

It was all she could do.

She opened the door and stepped inside with a forced smile. She found Tennille standing beside her fire and another woman spreading out fabric and other items on the little table beside the window. They both looked up as she entered, and Tennille's face lit up with a grin.

"Dearest Portia, how glad I am to see you!" her future sister-in-law laughed as she crossed the room and embraced her. "When my brother told me you were open to having my seamstress call after all, it was a happy day indeed. I hope you don't mind that I tagged along."

Portia shook her head. "Not at all. I am pleased to see you."

"May I present Miss King?" Tennille asked, holding a hand out to the other woman. "Probably the best mantua maker in all of England, so don't tell anyone else about her for fear they will drive her prices up and her availability down."

Miss King laughed and held out a hand. "A great pleasure, my lady. I hear we will also be fitting your mother for a gown for the wedding. Is she at home?"

Portia caught her breath and glanced at the two women. "I—well—"

"Lady Portia's mother is unwell," Tennille interrupted kindly. "And my understanding is that she may not be able to join us today."

"I would have to look in on her and ascertain her...fitness," Portia whispered, cheeks hot with a blush.

Miss King must have sensed the undercurrent, but made no indication. "I see. Of course it is best to have a true model by which to create a gown, but if she is unable to come down to be measured, I could also look at one of her current gowns and make something likely to fit very well."

Portia nearly drooped with relief. "That may be best, but I will check."

"Shall we start with you, though?" Miss King asked, motioning to a place by the light of the window. "I have a great many delicious fabrics that will suit your fair looks well."

Portia followed her to the table and found a pretty pile of fabric. Much of it seemed very appropriate for a wedding, but there were other selections that couldn't possibly be for that special day. Her confusion must have been reflected on her face, as Miss King smiled.

"Your future husband has asked that after I complete your wedding gown posthaste, I also create a full wardrobe of new gowns for you. So you will choose those fabrics today as well."

Portia gasped. "I—he—?"

"Don't question, my dear, just enjoy a new wardrobe," Tennille said with a squeeze of her arm.

Portia shook her head. If Miles already believed she had been part of a trick to capture him as a husband, the amount of money he was spending now had to bother him immensely. Would he even be speaking to her by the time they wed?

Tennille gave the seamstress a quick look, and the other woman smiled. "I realize I have left something in the carriage. Excuse me."

As she stepped from the room, Tennille touched Portia's arm. "Please don't look so forlorn, Portia."

Portia all but wailed. Could she do nothing right?

"I don't mean to. I appreciate all you and your brother are doing. Your kindness, especially given the circumstances, is entirely unexpected."

Tennille tilted her head. "Portia, there are two options in this world. We can make the best of our circumstances or we can fight them with every step. Perhaps the beginnings of this marriage you will enter with my brother are not the best, but I hope in time you will find some happiness together. That you will take your place in our family without lowering your chin or feeling the heat of a blush at the circumstances."

Portia let out a sigh. "Yes. I will try."

"Good." Tennille smiled over her shoulder as Miss King returned. "Now let us get you measured and pick some fabrics, shall we?"

Portia moved toward the table and the stunning array of beautiful things to be found there. Miles and his family continued to present her with kindness.

She could only hope it wouldn't run out once a ring had been put on her finger. And that the bargain she had made with Miles wouldn't break her in every way that was important.

Chapter Eight

The beautifully appointed carriage Miles had sent for Portia pulled up to the massive home right on the edges of St. James Park. Portia peeked around the curtain and sucked in a breath. It was huge. It was beautiful.

It was hers...*somehow.*

At least after tomorrow morning when she and Miles would be wed. Since the dress fitting a few days before, the final arrangements had been made, the last signings of contracts had been done and a few select invitations had been sent.

All without her seeing Miles for more than ten minutes all put together. Certainly without her spending any time alone with him.

She sighed as the footman opened the door and helped her out. There was a party tonight. One she wished she could avoid, but appearances were stressed to her daily by her brother.

She moved to the front door, which opened even before she reached it. A tall, very official-looking butler greeted her.

"Good evening, Lady Portia," he intoned in important tones as he allowed her into the warm parlor out of the frigid winter air. He took her wrap. "Lord Weatherfield awaits you in the blue parlor."

Portia blinked. She had not lived in a home with multiple parlors for so long, she hardly knew how to respond. "I see. Are the other guests already here?" she asked as she followed the man to the apparently blue parlor.

He glanced at her over his shoulder. "Other guests?" he repeated.

She nodded. "Yes."

The butler paused at the door and shook his head. "There are no other guests, my lady."

Before she could respond, he opened the door and announced her. Miles was standing by the fire and turned. "Thank you, Armstrong. Stay a moment, will you?"

The butler stepped aside and led her into a parlor that was quite blue indeed. The walls had a navy hue with bright white wainscoting and the furniture had hints of blue as well. She wondered, briefly, what lady had picked these designs...and hoped it was Tennille and not some mistress.

Miles interrupted her troubling thoughts by saying, "Portia, I would like to present my butler, Armstrong."

She turned and smiled. "Yes, thank you."

"You'll meet the other servants later, I'll present them the day after we are wed." Miles shrugged. "But Armstrong is a good sort, very accommodating, and he will make sure your things are put away once you are officially the lady of this house. He has also found a few candidates for a lady's maid for you, so you may interview them after we wed."

She looked at the butler with a start. She hadn't even thought of such a thing. "Oh...thank you. I hope it didn't put you out at all."

The servant appeared surprised for a moment. "It is no trouble, my lady. I certainly hope you will find the candidates satisfactory when you meet them next week." He glanced at Miles. "Will you require anything further, my lord?"

Miles shook his head. "Supper in two hours?"

"Yes, sir." The butler tilted his head toward her and then exited the room, closing the door behind himself.

Portia swallowed hard as she returned her attention to Miles. "I-I thought there would be others, but your butler said there were no other guests."

He tilted his head. "Are you disappointed?"

She couldn't answer that question. In truth, she had no idea how she felt. When she had been quiet for a moment, he smiled and moved on her a few steps.

"Now you remind me of how you were the first night I saw you at the masquerade. Silent. Would you like to nod or shake your head for me instead?"

Portia felt blood flood her cheeks. "You mock me," she whispered, tears stinging her eyes.

He moved on her again, his face gentle.

"Not at all." He was right on top of her now, his heat permeating her skin, his scent filling her and making her weak with what she now recognized was powerful desire. "I found you very fetching that night. I find you equally fetching now."

He reached out and cupped her cheek. She couldn't help but lean into his palm with a ragged sigh.

He swallowed and then stepped back.

"I brought you here with a purpose." He smiled. "Two purposes. The first is your mother."

The desire faded to the background and Portia swayed as fear overwhelmed her. "My mother?"

He caught her elbow to steady her. "Great God, Portia, sit." He urged her to the settee and took a place beside her. He stroked her hand. "I didn't mean to frighten you. I only wanted to tell you the arrangements I made with your brother."

"Which were?" she asked, blinking rapidly because the fear would not subside, no matter how much he reassured her.

"He will release her to my custody," he said softly and released her hand to stand. "In fact, he seemed eager to do so."

Portia flinched at the tightness in his voice. "At what price?"

He hesitated too long before he shook his head. "Do not worry yourself."

She squeezed her eyes shut. His silence must mean a great deal indeed. Which her brother would squander, no doubt.

"I cannot help but worry, Miles. You have already been forced into this situation and now it becomes more and more difficult and expensive for you." She shook her head slowly. "You must despise me, though you are too kind to outright tell me so."

His brow wrinkled. "Far from it."

She stared at him, trying to stay strong, trying not to allow the tears she felt stinging her eyes to fall. She didn't want to play on his emotions in that way, not after everything else.

"How could you not?"

He leaned in, taking both her hands. "You transfer your brother's cold regard to me, Portia, but you will learn that I am not like him."

Portia steadied her breath, difficult to do when he was touching her, when his face was so close to hers. "Will my mother stay in our current home?"

"Great God, no. That hovel isn't fit for rats." She flinched, but he didn't stop speaking. "No. In Town, she will have a wing in this home. I can show you if you'd like. And in my country estate, she'll have a cottage on the estate. Somewhere she can have privacy...and so can we."

Her eyes went wide. "You would bring her here to your home? Even knowing that she has caused...*scenes* that might be embarrassing to you?"

He shrugged. "We will handle that problem if it comes up, but I intend to provide her with a sympathetic companion whose only duty will be to watch her and tend to her needs."

Portia covered her mouth. "Potts and I were just talking about how much that would help her."

"I'm sure it would," Miles agreed. "In fact, I wonder if your housekeeper herself might wish to take that position since she appears to have affection for your mother and she will be out of a job otherwise. Somehow I doubt your brother will provide her with any kind of reference worth having."

"Potts," Portia whispered, but she didn't have to ponder the question. Potts would take that position gladly and be very good at it. "Yes, I think she would be a wonderful choice."

Portia nodded and Miles smiled. "Excellent, I will broach the subject with her as soon as I can."

He seemed to be ready to continue talking, but he suddenly stopped and stared at her.

"What is it?" he asked, his brow wrinkling. "Why do you look at me that way?"

Portia licked her suddenly dry lips. "You—you cannot know what this means to me, Miles. To know I will no longer have to worry about my mother and her safety. To feel she is protected." She sucked in a breath. "It is a gift greater than any I could have asked for."

She didn't think about what she was about to do. She simply did it out of instinct, out of loneliness, out of a deep desire to give Miles something, anything.

She leaned into him, wrapped her arms around his neck and kissed him.

Miles stood stunned as Portia's lips collided with his. But he couldn't deny how powerfully he reacted. Her technique was artless, innocent, but there was simmering passion in her touch that could not be denied. He wrapped his arms around her waist and drew her closer as he tilted his head and parted his lips to taste her.

She hesitated, and he drew back to look down at her. She had a dazed look on her face that both intrigued and troubled him. He didn't release her, but he whispered, "Portia, I don't wish for you to do things you don't want to do in order to repay a debt I do not place upon you."

His voice was rough with need he doubted...or hoped...she didn't fully understand.

She blinked, and he waited for her to extract herself from his embrace, but she didn't. She simply looked up at him, her lip trembling, her warm body still in his arms.

"I cannot tell you that I am doing something I don't wish for with all my heart."

The soft power of those words had blood flowing to a rapidly hardening cock. One that wished to be buried to the hilt in the flexing wetness of her slit.

"But," she continued, her gaze darting away. "I also cannot tell you that my kiss isn't offered as a repayment of a debt. A gift to somehow match yours, though it can never mean as much to you as what you are doing does to me. But my kiss, my body...it's all I have. So won't you take something from me in order to balance the discrepancy your kindness has created?"

Once again, the faint gentlemanly urges deep within Miles whispered to him to release this woman. To stop himself from taking advantage of the offer she made after a lifetime of cruelty from other men.

But that voice was very quiet and easily squashed by another, louder one. One that told him not to take as she suggested, but to give. To bring this woman pleasure so powerful that she was weak in his arms and even more ready for the debauchery he intended to entertain once she was his wife.

"You are a temptation I never expected," he drawled as he lowered her to her back on the settee. "How could I have never seen it before?"

"No one saw me," she murmured, and he saw a flash of pain in her gaze before she turned it away.

"Well, I see you now. So very clearly," he growled before his mouth was on her a second time.

This time he didn't hesitate. He didn't allow her to innocently lead him. He claimed her with his tongue, sucking at her, swirling around her, tasting her and reveling in how his arousal increased with every single kiss. Reveling even more in how she shuddered with surrender after a mere moment in his arms.

He would have to be very careful if he didn't want to go too far before they wed. And for some reason, he didn't. Taking her was a pleasure he wanted to savor after a vicar pronounced them man and wife.

He drew a breath of calm and then put a bit of space between them. Just enough that he could allow his hand to travel down the length of her body. He smoothed his palm over her breasts, and she gasped, just as she had at the Donville Masquerade when he touched her similarly. He could still feel her pebbled nipples on his tongue and hear her soft moans of pleasure.

He would have them again tonight.

"I want to do something, Portia," he explained even as he caught a handful of her skirt and began to inch it up her body. "Will you allow it?"

He saw a shadow cross over her face. A brief moment where she questioned him, doubted him, but then she shook it away.

"I told you before and I repeated it tonight...I am yours in any way you like if you will help me. You have, and I won't renege on my part of the bargain."

He frowned at her blunt terms, but continued to lift her skirt. Soon enough she wouldn't see his touch as a duty. He knew very well that she was responsive, that she could be brought to release with his hands.

Now he wanted to try the same experiment with his tongue.

He sat up and looked at her. Her dress was hiked to her thighs, revealing worn stockings and a long expanse of legs he could imagine wrapped around his waist as he took her in 1 urgent strokes.

Later. Later.

For now he pressed his palms into those creamy thighs, urging them open as he held her gaze. Her body trembled, but she didn't resist as he made a space for himself between her legs and leaned in. There were three inches of silken fabric covering her sex, and he slid them up to rest on her belly before he looked at her again.

Through the slit in her drawers, he saw a hint of pink flesh. Wet, pink flesh that glistened in tempting and teasing fashion.

"I'm taking these off," he said, putting his fingers into the waist of her undergarments. "Don't wear them again."

Her eyes went wide. "Ever?"

"Never. I never want to lift your skirt and find your body covered again unless it is by something I give to you to wear." He held her stare. "Do you understand?"

She nodded, a jerky motion though he couldn't tell if she was utterly offended or completely aroused. Perhaps a touch of both.

He tossed the drawers away and sucked in breath through his teeth. He had touched her pussy in the carriage but not seen it. Now it was spread open to him like a fine meal and he forced himself to stay calm. To move slowly.

He looked up at her face. Her cheeks were dark red and she was shaking, but she didn't flinch. She didn't tell him to stop. He admired that strength. That dedication to the course she had put herself on.

"Don't be ashamed of your body," he said. "Not with me."

"No one has ever seen me this way," she whispered.

He flinched, thinking again of the fact that she was looking for Windbury that night at the masquerade. Had no one merely *seen* her this way or was she truly untouched?

"You are beautiful," he reassured her. "You look good enough to eat."

She swallowed, and he could see the wheels of her mind turning, turning, turning.

"Eat?" she repeated.

He nodded. "Surely you saw this at the masquerade. Saw the women being licked and pleasured?"

She let out a tiny moan and then nodded. "I-I saw them."

"Didn't you wonder what it would feel like to have a man's tongue on your skin? To feel him drive it deep inside of you? To taste you?"

Her nipples were getting hard beneath her dress, and he smiled. She was an apt pupil indeed.

"Answer me," he ordered softly.

She nodded again. "I wondered."

"Then let me show you," he said, and lowered his head between her legs. He rubbed his cheek against her inner thigh, inspiring a hiss of air from her lungs before he spread her lower lips with his thumbs and licked her from top to bottom with the flat of his tongue.

She arched beneath him with a wail of both surprise and pleasure that echoed in the room around them. Once again, he was nearly overwhelmed with a desire to drive his cock deep within her, but he controlled it. Tempered it. Reminded himself that soon he would do just that.

For now, though, he focused on her sex. He licked her again, tasting her sweetness, feeling it flood his mouth as she grew wet with his attentions. She arched beneath him, her eyes wide as he swirled his tongue around the swollen pearl of her clitoris.

"Miles," she gasped, and he smiled as he looked up the length of her quivering body without slowing the pace of his mouth on her wet slit.

She was writhing, her cheeks pink, though not from embarrassment this time, and her face contorted with pleasure. He pushed her legs open even farther and began to suck on her clitoris, swirling his tongue over the little nub with just the right pressure.

She cried out as her body began to convulse beneath him. She moaned as she turned her face into the settee cushions, her hips lifting toward him in a silent, reflexive demand for more. A demand he met as he dragged her through release until her body shook and she lay limp and panting on the pillows.

He licked her one last time, then sat up to smile at her. She was staring, eyes glassy with dazed desire, up at him.

"Do you feel like you have repaid some of my, as you put it, kindness?" he asked, stroking his fingers along her thighs slowly. His cock felt so hard that he could have driven it through a wall.

But he knew the wait would make the ultimate pleasure all the better.

She blinked at him. "That isn't all, though. You have taken no pleasure."

He shrugged. "Seeing you lose control is very much a pleasure."

She sat up enough that she leaned on her elbows, though she made no motion to fix herself. "You know that isn't what I mean. You give me release and take none for yourself. How can that put me in any position except that I continue to owe you more and more?"

With a frown, he reached up and pulled her skirts back over her body before he stood and paced away. Her utter lack of faith in him was troubling, especially when coupled with her surrender of her body. Most women of his acquaintance couldn't give themselves without faith in their partners at the very least.

It left him once again questioning everything he knew about the woman who would be his bride in only a few short hours.

"If you spend your life counting what you are owed and what you owe, you will never be happy, Portia," he said softly. "We are in this situation now and we can make the best of it or not. It's up to you what that answer is. One way or another, we will be wed tomorrow. Now, would you like to take a brief tour of the wing we have prepared for your mother?"

She got to her feet, watching him with continued wariness but also a hint of chagrin. Then she smoothed her wrinkled dress and reached for his arm.

"Yes. I would very much like to see what you have in store for my mother."

He nodded once and led her from the room, but as he guided her upstairs, he was struck by how little had been resolved by their encounter. He wanted her all the more, but Portia was still an unexpected mystery he feared he might never solve.

Chapter Nine

It was her wedding day. Those words echoed in her head, repeating over and over until she thought she would go mad with it. But there was no pretending this moment away now. It was far too late for that.

Portia stood in the hallway of Miles' home, staring through the open door to the ballroom where her fiancé was located, his broad back to her. A few friends and family members, including her fidgeting mother, sat along aisles, awaiting her entry that would signal the beginning of the wedding.

Her knees trembled. She had hardly slept after leaving Miles' home the night before. She had not eaten that morning. She kept thinking about his touch, his bringing her pleasure, the bargain they had made about sex and sin.

She had no idea what her marriage would be like, but she had no doubt it was going to change her life forever.

Everything felt like a dream as her brother took her arm and glanced down at her. "Are you ready?"

She flinched at his tone. Hammond sounded so pleased to be rid of her, so happy that this moment had arrived, no matter how they had come to this place.

"I have no choice but to be ready," she responded, trying to maintain composure. "So we should begin."

Her brother did not kiss her cheek, he did not even look at her as they began to walk into the room together, down the long expanse of the decorated ballroom and toward Miles.

Miles turned as they hit the halfway point of the room, and Portia saw him catch his breath a little. She wished she could read his thoughts. Know if he thought she looked pretty in her gorgeous new gown, which had been finished only that morning, or whether he was just trying to keep himself from fleeing the room screaming.

She turned her attention to the others in the room. On her side of the aisle, her mother sat, blinking a little too much as she clung to Mrs. Potts' hand. But she was smiling and that warmed Portia's heart immensely. At least she could save her mother.

Ava and Christian were there too, also smiling, though Portia recognized Ava's hesitation. And then there was Hammond's wife, Iris. Her arms were folded and she watched Portia like a bird of prey would do. She briefly wondered if Iris would swoop at her if she were to try to run.

On Miles' side of the aisle were just his sister and brother-in-law. Tennille watched her with unfettered kindness and an utter lack of hesitation. For some reason, Portia was welcome with them, though she certainly had not earned that place of friendship with Miles' family.

Portia's thoughts vanished as she reached Miles. Her brother took her hand and placed it in Miles' before he stepped back to take his place beside his own wife.

The clergyman began to talk. He droned on, speaking about the purpose of marriage. When he reached the point where he spoke of how marriage was a remedy against sin and fornication, Portia stiffened. She wasn't certain her own marriage would prevent either. Nor was she entirely convinced she wished to be free of those things if they made her feel so good.

She shivered and tried to attend to the rest of the ceremony. It passed mercifully swiftly, and soon he said, "Those whom God hath joined together, let no man put asunder."

There was a resounding amen and it was over. She was a wife. And not just any wife, but wife to one of the most celebrated rakes in London, whom a dozen women had tried to capture. She was Marchioness Weatherfield.

Her knees shook, and she clung to Miles' strong arm as he led her from the ballroom and back to a parlor where they would gather themselves before they met everyone else for the wedding breakfast.

As he shut the door, she moved to the other side of the room and stared at him. She had no idea what to say. How to say it. How to face him as a wife.

He seemed to have no such hesitation. He crossed the room in three long steps and gathered her into his arms. His mouth was on hers, heated and passionate. He claimed her with his tongue and her body lit on fire. She couldn't control the needy moan which escaped her lips as she clung to him, shaking with desire and the knowledge that in a few short hours he would take her body and they would truly be bound forever.

He pulled back, his eyes wild, and smoothed his jacket. "Good morning, wife."

She smiled despite all her worries and fears. "Good day, husband."

He grinned in return and for a moment their eyes locked. She saw emotions in his stare, lightness she hadn't noticed before when she saw him as merely a friend, before she'd felt the full impact of his desire.

"They are gathering in the Blue Parlor," he said with a shake of his head. "So I suppose we must join them."

She tensed. "The Blue Parlor where last night...where you and I..."

Blood flooded her cheeks and he smiled again, flashing straight white teeth she had felt scrape along her—

"No one but us knows what we did in that room," Miles drawled. "Consider it the first of many sinful secrets we shall share."

Many sinful secrets. Portia shivered.

"Now come along, Lady Weatherfield," Miles continued. "Your guests are waiting."

"So you are wed."

Portia turned away from the sidebar lined with wine and smiled as Ava wrapped an arm around her. She leaned into her friend and for a moment she was allowed to be herself. To be *real*.

"I am, it seems," she said with a shake of her head. "Good Lord."

Ava poured them each a glass of wine. "Are you well?"

"I am as well as can be expected under the circumstances." Portia laughed to soften the words. "Do not misunderstand me, I am not complaining. This entire fiasco is my own fault and I could do far worse than Miles, who has been nothing but kind to me."

Ava's face relaxed a touch. "I'm glad to hear it. You certainly look lovely."

Portia looked down at herself. It had been so long since she had such a pretty frock that she found herself secretly fingering the silken folds when she hoped no one was looking.

"His sister's lady's maid arrived at my home and helped me and my mother ready ourselves," Portia explained. "And the gown is one of several her seamstress made with some kind of magic, considering how lovely they are and how quickly they were sewn. Apparently there are to be a dozen more coming in the next month or so. All arranged for and paid for by *him*, of course."

She glanced at Miles. He was talking to his sister and her husband. His face was utterly neutral, she couldn't tell what he thought or felt. Nor had she been able to since the moment they joined the larger group. It was almost as if that searing kiss and that whispered promise of passion in the parlor had never happened.

Would she ever solve the puzzle of her...*husband*?

"Why should he not shower you with pretty things meant to make you light up?" Ava said with a smile. "You are his wife now."

"Plenty of men do not do so. Especially to wives they did not choose." Portia sighed.

Ava's eyebrows lifted. "I can understand your hesitation, but you must expect the best. He's taking care of your mother. Did he do that because of my suggestion that you..." She leaned closer. "Offer yourself in exchange?"

Portia hesitated. This was hardly a subject to broach in the middle of a parlor, not an hour after her marriage. But she so desperately wanted to talk to Ava about it.

She turned into her friend to block the rest of the room from what they were saying. "I did. And he accepted those terms."

"Excellent." Ava clasped her hands together with a wicked smile.

Portia shook her head in confusion. "*Excellent?* How is this anything close to that?"

"You underestimate the power of passion," her friend murmured with a quick, heated glance toward her own husband, across the room kindly entertaining Portia's mother and Potts.

"That may be because I have no idea what to do!" Portia said with a sigh. "Miles implies a large array of passions, shocking and powerful. Already he has, er, *done things* to me."

"Well, that is how you two ended up here," her friend laughed, her attention still on Christian.

Portia shook her head. "Not that."

Ava's eyes went wide and suddenly she was staring at Portia. "Since you two were compromised at the masquerade?"

Portia swallowed, her hands shaking as she thought of the pleasurable moments she and Miles had shared in the carriage and even in this very room. Her body thrummed with desire just recalling them.

"Yes," she whispered.

"And has he..." Ava dropped her voice. "Taken you?"

Blood rushed to Portia's cheeks, making them almost unbearably hot. "Not taken me, but...*other* pleasures."

The corners of Ava's lips lifted slightly. "That is very encouraging."

"Encouraging?" Portia repeated, forcing her voice to stay low even though she wanted to shake her friend in frustration. "How so? As I have already said, I have no idea how to keep his attention or fulfill his no-doubt high expectations."

Ava smiled. "You will learn quickly enough, I will tell you that. When a man desires you and you desire him in return, what to do becomes very, very natural, very quickly."

"I have a hard time believing you." Portia shivered. Nothing she and Miles did felt natural. Uncommonly pleasureable, yes. Natural, no. "Can't you give me advice beyond 'do what comes naturally'?"

Ava touched her arm. "I can certainly give you advice," she whispered. "As delicately as I can in this environment. But are you certain you wish to hear what I have to say?"

Portia took a deep breath. This was her only chance before her wedding night to have a talk with someone who understood. In the public of a parlor or not, she couldn't turn that down.

"Yes," she said, leaning closer with nervousness and excitement mobbing her. "Tell me everything you can before we are interrupted."

Miles kept a tight, false smile on his face, but it was a difficult proposition as he mingled with the few guests from his wedding and a few more who had been invited to the wedding breakfast after the ceremony ended. Talking to them, accepting their felicitations, seeing their knowing smiles behind their fans was almost unbearable.

If someone had told him a fortnight ago that he would be wed after a scandal, he would have laughed in their face.

And yet here he was.

"Weatherfield!"

He turned, and his smile wavered as Portia's brother approached. Cosslow had a huge grin on his face and a drink in his hand. He was wobbling ever so slightly, a result of draining Miles' bar since the moment the wedding ceremony had come to a close.

How in the world had he ever called this bastard a friend?

"Cosslow," Miles said with a slight nod as acknowledgment.

"It all went off without a hitch." Cosslow hiccupped. "I must say I feared you might go running off, damn the consequences. Not that anyone would blame you."

Miles flinched at the cruelty of both his new brother-in-law's words and his tone.

"I had no intention of doing that to your sister," he said. "I'm a man of my word."

"Yes, so it appears." Hammond shrugged.

The two of them looked across the room at Portia. She stood with Lady Rothcastle and the two of them had their heads close together, talking with far more intensity than Miles would have expected at a wedding celebration.

"Ava has certainly changed for the better with *her* marriage," Hammond mused with a guttural grunt of appreciation. "Who knew?"

Miles pursed his lips in disgust. "They have been friends a long time, have they not?"

"She and Portia?" Hammond shrugged. "As long as I can recall. But then, the wallflowers always seem to stick together."

Miles sighed. "Their friendship seems deeper than that."

Cosslow looked at him almost as if he didn't understand the statement.

"I suppose it is." He swigged a drink. "Portia used to moon over Ava's brother, though Windbury never showed her any more mind than any other man did."

Miles tensed. Once again, there was a stark reminder that Portia apparently cared for another man. She had all but admitted it the first night they met at the masquerade. And she had been seeking another man the second night before they fell into each other's arms.

His stomach turned. Was that what the two friends were talking about so closely? *Liam?*

A sudden, mind-numbing possessiveness passed through him, overtook him. This was his wife. *His.* And he would by God claim her in some way right now if only to take thoughts of another man from her mind.

"Excuse me," he muttered, barely acknowledging Cosslow as he set his drink down on the closest table and strode across the parlor toward Portia and Ava. Portia's back was to him, but Ava saw him before he reached the two. Her eyes went wide, and he realized she recognized his intent.

She shook Portia's arm just as he reached them. Portia turned toward him and that possessive need to claim her was multiplied as she stared up at him, brown eyes wide, lips parted. In a pretty gown with her hair done properly, she looked more beautiful than ever. And he wanted her so much that his groin ached and he could only hope that desire wasn't too obvious to the entire room.

"I would like to talk to you," he managed to growl out through clenched teeth.

Her brow wrinkled. "Miles—" she began.

He caught her elbow. "Now. In private," he said, tossing Ava a glare. "Lady Rothcastle, do excuse us."

Ava shook her head, a wry smile on her face. "Oh, of course, my lord."

He ignored her knowing tone and guided Ava from the parlor and down the hall to his office. He hauled her inside and slammed the door, locking it behind himself with suddenly shaking hands.

He smoothed his jacket before he turned to look at her. She was standing in the middle of his office, staring at him as if he had sprouted a second head.

"Miles," she whispered, and he groaned. Every time she said his damn name it made his desire deepen. "What have I done to displease you?"

He shut his eyes. There were so many answers to that question. Thinking about another man displeased him. Remaining uncertain of her innocence displeased him. Her not being naked and under him displeased him.

"Miles?" she repeated, daring to come a step closer as she searched his face with questioning brown eyes.

He reached for her, catching her hand and hauling her against him in one smooth motion. She gasped as their bodies collided, but the sound was lost as his mouth crushed hers. His control was lost seconds later, and he maneuvered her to perch on the edge of his desk.

He pulled away, his face inches from hers, and held her stare.

"You are mine, Portia. Do you understand that?"

She swallowed hard and then nodded slowly.

"Whatever happened before," he continued as he unlaced her dress along the back. "You are mine now. And I'm going to prove it to you here and now."

Chapter Ten

Portia could hardly breathe as Miles stripped her pretty gown away. She expected him to toss it aside in his hurry, but instead he placed it gently across the back of a chair before he turned back to her.

His gaze was dark and hooded, but even she, innocent as she remained, could not deny the heavy, heated desire there. He wanted her. But would he truly claim her as his wife in his office with their wedding guests not ten feet away?

She didn't know whether to be fearful of that idea or utterly titillated by it.

He looked her up and down, and suddenly he smiled.

"You listened," he murmured as he stepped forward, parting her legs to stand between them as she perched precariously on his desk.

"Listened?" she panted, hardly able to think.

He reached between them and placed the flat of his palm on her wet and tingling sex. "You aren't wearing drawers."

She swallowed as the heel of his palm ground into her and stole her ability to form coherent sentences. "Yes..." she gasped, struggling. "I...did as you...asked me."

The last word trailed out on a moan as pleasure mobbed her.

"Great God, you are responsive," he muttered, almost more to himself than to her.

"Only because you make me so," she panted, dipping her head over her shoulders as her breath caught again and again.

How could he do this to her with just his touch? How could he make her shake and beg and moan like a wanton? Her legs shook and her nipples hardened, scraping against the soft, silky fabric of her new chemise. She felt utterly aware of not only her own breath, her own body, but of his. She wanted to feel him against her.

Ava had told her, in their brief but heated conversation, that all she had to do was ask for what she desired.

She drew back and stared up at him. He met her gaze and her stomach clenched as need ratcheted up.

"Please, please," she began, blushing as she grasped for his waist and pulled him closer. "I want...I want—"

"What do you want?" he asked, voice low and rough. "Tell me what you want."

"You," she admitted finally. "Just you to touch me. I want to feel what you do to me."

His eyes widened, but then his mouth turned up in a possessive grin.

"Oh, you will," he promised as he pulled her hips closer and wrapped her legs behind his back.

She felt something hard there, something rubbing her trembling sex through his trousers. His member, if the drawings that had aroused her years ago and the images from the night of the masquerade were correct. He would put that inside of her to make her his in every way.

She wanted that now. More than anything.

"Are you going to take me?" she whispered, lifting herself against him in an effort to feel the pleasure she knew was coming.

"Here? In my office?" he asked.

She nodded, gasping when he rocked forward and the hardness that was still covered rubbed her perfectly.

"No. Not here, not like this. In a few hours everyone will leave and I will take you to my bed and I will press this—" he took her hand and put that hard member against her fingers, "—deep within you until you cry out with pleasure you have never known. But for now, I only want to remind you that you are mine. And that I can have you anywhere, anytime, including when our parlor is filled with guests, wondering where we've gone."

A groan escaped her lips at that naughty thought.

"Some of them will know," he continued, pressing his hand against her again. His fingers breeched her now and he began to curl them gently within her. "They'll know that we are succumbing to desire. They'll guess that you are here, with me, your legs spread while I bury myself inside of you." He drove his fingers deep. "Like this."

She arched her back as pleasure began to build, steady and swift, in her clenching sheath. But this time it wasn't enough. She wanted more, she wanted him, all of him, some of him, any of him.

"What about me?" she gasped as she reached out to stroke the hardness hidden within the folds of his trousers. "What will they think I am doing to you?"

His gaze jerked to hers, and he stared at her for a moment. Then he unfastened his trousers and pulled the hard length of his member free.

She stared. She had never been so close to a naked man before. Even at the masquerade, she had only watched from the corner of her eye. Now he was here, his body inches from hers, her fingers near him. She could feel the heat radiating from his body and see the strain as he leaned in to her.

"They would guess you are taking my cock with your body," he whispered, wrapping her fingers around him. "That I am stroking inside of you as you beg me for more."

She moaned as he began to move his fingers faster inside of her. He was stroking her toward release and she found herself doing the same with him. Her hand moved over him in the same rhythm as he moved inside of her. His hips began to jerk as she cried out, and she was lost.

Her body rocked out of control as wave after wave of intense release flowed through her. She gasped as she continued to stroke his...he had called it his cock...and then, to her surprise, he grunted her name and his essence flowed from his body between them.

For a moment, they stayed like that, his fingers inside of her, her hand around him, staring at each other as they panted in mutual release. Then he glided his fingers from her sheath and smiled.

"The next time you open your legs for me, it will be for my cock," he said, pulling from her grasp gently and yanking his trousers up around his naked flesh. "Be ready."

She quivered at that sensual promise and the dark and dangerous look in his eyes as he pulled a handkerchief from his pocket and gave it to her to wipe her hands. There was the dichotomy of him again. He was an animal bent on having her in any and every way his wicked mind could imagine. And yet he could be kind, he could be thoughtful, as he was when he gave her a cloth to wipe off her hands or had dresses made for her or did something to help her mother.

How she would ever come to fully understand him, she did not know.

She turned to find him holding her gown out for her. "Allow me to assist you," he said and helped her as she stepped back into the pretty dress.

He was as skillful at buttoning it as he had been at loosening it and soon she was fixed, as though this moment between them had never even happened. She glanced at her hair in a mirror above his sidebar and shook her head. She looked exactly the same as she had before they left the parlor, only a little flushed.

"Ready to return and pretend this never happened?" he asked with a low chuckle that made her still-tingling sex clench with need once again.

What in the world was he doing to her?

"Y-Yes," she stammered as she took the elbow he offered and they left his office to return to the parlor. When she touched him, the tension crackled between them and she forced herself to take a long breath.

"You are very pink," he said, close to her ear as they moved toward the open parlor door.

She looked up at him with a shake of her head. "Do you not wish to take responsibility for that?"

He chuckled as they entered the room. "I'm more than pleased to take responsibility," he said as he released her. "Now go and be hostess. And think of what will happen when all these interlopers are gone and you and I are alone in my bed."

She staggered slightly as she walked away from him, past Ava and her knowing smile, toward a small group of revelers who she had not yet met with since the ceremony.

But she couldn't stop thinking of exactly the image Miles had put into her mind. Of his bed, of his cock and of the moment when she would finally be completely and irrevocably claimed.

Miles loosened his cravat and tossed his jacket on the chair beside the roaring fire before he moved to the small sideboard in his chamber and poured himself a strong drink. He had been married for eleven hours. Eleven hours filled with breakfasts and parties and family luncheons and visitors and well-wishers and an early supper he couldn't eat fast enough so that everyone would simply go home and leave him to Portia.

Portia, who he hadn't even thought of until she was revealed as his obsession. Portia, who he now dreamed of claiming day and night.

A dream that would come true as soon as she saw her exhausted mother settled in her new set of chambers far across the house.

He did not begrudge her those moments with Lady Cosslow, but he did wish they would pass faster.

As if his wishes had been granted, there was a light knock on the door behind him and he turned as Armstrong opened the door.

"Lady Weatherfield, my lord," he said.

Miles smiled. It was the first and only time his wife would be escorted to his chambers as if she were a visitor.

"Thank you, Armstrong, that will be all."

The butler nodded and stepped away to reveal Portia. Her hands were clenched together in front of her, her face was pink and her eyes darted around his chamber as she remained in the doorway, waiting.

"Will you come in?" he pressed, motioning her inside.

She jumped, as if she had forgotten she was standing stock-still in the hallway, and nodded as she stepped inside. "Of course, how silly of me."

"Close the door," he demanded, using all his self-control to remain in one place and not charge on her like an aroused bull.

She hesitated ever so slightly and then reached behind her to do as he requested. When the door clicked shut, she jumped.

"Have you seen your chamber yet?" he asked.

She shook her head. "N-no. With all the excitement today, I have not."

He motioned to the door. "It is through here."

He moved there and opened it. She walked to stand beside him and peeked into the room. No fire had been lit there and it was dark.

She laughed, the tension broken by the sound. "I'm sure it is lovely."

He smiled with her. "It is, I assure you. And you will see it fully tomorrow morning. But tonight, we will adjourn to the other room."

He pointed to the door that led to his bedroom.

"Yes," she murmured and her eyes went impossibly wide.

"In a moment," he added. "Would you like a drink first?"

She swallowed hard, then nodded. "Yes."

"Brandy?" he asked, holding up his own glass.

She nodded again. "Please."

When he handed her a glass a moment later, he was surprised as she downed the entire portion in one heaving gulp. He stared at her, eyebrows lifted.

"Are you well?" he asked.

She blushed as she set the empty glass aside. "I admit my nerves are shaken. It has been a...a very trying day."

"Sit," he urged, pointing to the chairs by the fire.

She took the one that did not contain his jacket and clenched her hands in her lap. He took the other, leaning forward to take her hand before he spoke again.

"How did you find your mother?" he asked, massaging the palm of her right hand.

She shivered at the touch. "Well," she croaked out. "Thank you. She is settling nicely into her new quarters, and Mrs. Potts takes very good care of her."

"Excellent. I'm certain she will have a period of adjustment, but I want her and you to know that she is most welcome here."

Portia tilted her head and for a moment he saw a flash of deep pain in her stare. "Why?"

He blinked. "I don't understand."

"I know that you and I agreed to a bargain, my utter surrender in exchange for your help, but you do not have to be so kind to her. Why are you?"

"You are so accustomed to the unkindness of others that you refuse to believe it," he said softly, watching as the firelight danced off her face. "Portia, I do not love you. You do not love me. That is not why our match was made, so we do not need to pretend it has anything to do with what we are."

She didn't react to that statement, for negative or positive, so he continued.

"But you *are* my wife now. And I will treat you with kindness and generosity because you deserve to be treated no less. Our bargain aside, you do not need to live in fear of me or worry that my kindness is fickle."

She pondered that a moment. "Are you saying we could become...friends?"

"Yes." He smiled. "That would be my greatest hope. That a friendship will bloom between us from the warmth we already share."

She pressed her lips together. "It is the most we could hope for, I suppose."

He wrinkled his brow at the faraway tone to her voice. Slowly, he stood and held out a hand. "That and passion."

She stared up at him, lips slightly parted. "That and passion," she repeated.

"Which I will make sure you experience as often as we both have an interest in it. I will give you pleasures that you have never imagined."

As she placed her fingers in his, he drew her to her feet. Slowly, he lowered his mouth to hers and brushed his lips back and forth against hers. She relaxed, sighing into his mouth as her arms came around his neck and her body molded to his. He drew back reluctantly.

"Come to my room," he whispered, shocked by how broken and needy his tone was. "Come to my bed. Now."

Chapter Eleven

Portia trembled as she followed Miles through what felt like a very ominous door. Once inside, she took a breath as she looked around the room.

His bedchamber was darkly designed and intensely masculine both in color and décor. It had a huge bed against the wall opposite the door. A roaring fire danced in a massive fireplace, warming the room and searing her already heated flesh. He had a few pieces of fine furniture scattered around the room, but her eyes came back, again and again, to that bed.

That damn bed.

Her gaze slipped to Miles, who had shut the door separating the sitting room from the bedchamber and was leaning against it, staring at her. He was devastatingly handsome, his shirt collar loosened, his hair mussed, one foot folded over the other. His dark stare bore into her, daring her to run or defy him.

She had no intention of doing either.

Instead she turned her back to him and motioned to the line of buttons which closed her gown.

"You have already proven your deft fingers in more ways than one today. Will you unfasten me?" she asked softly, shocked by her own boldness. What was happening to her? What was he doing to her?

There was a moment's breath of hesitation, but then he moved behind her, his hands gliding to her shoulders. She leaned into his touch with a shuddering sigh, one that grew louder as he unfastened the first button at the top of her gown.

She waited for him to move to the second, but instead he pressed his lips to the tiny sliver of flesh he had revealed. A shock of sensation shot from the place where he touched her and settled between her thighs, where her sex began to throb madly.

"How do you do this to me?" she whispered as he unhooked the second button and allowed his mouth to move down her bared flesh.

"What do I do?" he asked before he moved his attention to the third button. His breath brushed her ear, and she shivered with pleasure and need. "Tell me."

"You make me...*weak*," she moaned, for he was parting her gown now, opening a great expanse of flesh to his tongue, his lips, his rough fingertips.

And as he touched her, she also realized she had been sleeping until he put his hands on her at the masquerade. And now she was awake and she wanted more and more of him.

He unhooked two buttons at a time now, slipping his hands beneath her chemise to caress her skin.

"Be weak to me," he urged as he slipped those hands through the loose folds of her gown and touched her bare breasts beneath her chemise. "Lose control for me. Give me all that you are and all that you desire and I swear to you, you will never be sorry."

He pulled her back against his chest, his thumbs strumming her sensitive nipples, his mouth against the side of her neck. Portia's vision was beginning to blur, the room spinning as she spiraled into a fog of desire.

"Yes," she panted. "Anything you want. Anything."

He pushed the dress away and it pooled at her feet, leaving her in only her short chemise that just brushed the top of her thighs. Without her drawers, her naked backside pressed against the front of his trousers and she felt the outline of his hardness against the smooth globes of her bottom.

He returned his hands to her breasts, this time on top of the silky fabric. He began to massage in slow circles, dragging the chemise across her nipples with purposeful slowness. Deep within her she felt an ache growing, a deep and driving need that throbbed between her legs and made it hard to breathe, hard to think, hard to do anything except grind back against Miles in some ancient, ingrained need to be possessed.

He grunted as she moved against him and then he dragged her back even harder to mold her to his body.

"Careful," he whispered close to her ear. "Be certain you know what you're doing."

She almost laughed. She had *no* idea what she was doing—she had only a few explicit suggestions from Ava and her own heated wants to guide her. But even though Miles told her to be wary, his rough tone and the way he sucked along her neck told her she was doing something very, very right.

She took a deep breath and rolled her hips against him once more. He cursed beneath his breath and spun her around to face him, crushing his mouth against hers as he backed her toward the bed on the opposite side of the room.

Her heart raced as her backside hit the edge. She reached a hand back and steadied herself as he pulled away from the searing kiss and stared at her.

"I'm going to enjoy this," he murmured as he reached up and stripped the buttons of his shirt open in one swift motion. She gasped as he shrugged the fine linen fabric away to flutter to the floor behind him.

Though she'd had far more experience in the past few days than ever before in the male form, nothing could have prepared her for this. For Miles, standing before her, shirtless.

He was a god, crafted from marble, made in the image of something utterly perfect. He had broad shoulders, muscles rippling down his stomach and trim hips that disappeared into dangerously low-slung trousers. He was lean and strong, and she had the strangest urge to drag her nails down his skin, to lick him like he was icing on a cake, to rub on him like a cat begging to be petted.

He reached out and put a finger beneath her chin. "Close your mouth, wife."

She blinked for the first time in what felt like a long time and shook her head in sudden embarrassment.

Of course she would make an idiot of herself, staring at a man who was so far above her that she never would have even shared a hint of a chance with him had he not been forced into this position. His perfection reminded her of that fact and now any boldness dissipated from her body and left her shifting with uneasiness.

"How disappointed you must be in your bargain," she whispered, fighting the urge to cover herself, to turn her face away. It was *only* the agreement they had made about the protection of her mother that kept her rooted in her spot.

His brow wrinkled. "Why on earth would you say such a foolish thing, Portia?"

She shrugged, trying to downplay how silly she felt, how much this moment was a reminder of cold reality.

"You are beautiful," she whispered. "You could have any woman in London, probably any woman in the world. And I? I am a spinster who never was more than passably pretty in certain lights. What a step down for you."

He caught her chin, tilting her face up so she couldn't look away. His eyes bore into her with an intensity that was equal to the leaping, glowing fire behind him.

"You listen to me, Portia. I cannot tell you that I longed for you for years as we passed each other in ballrooms. Or that men drooled at the mere thought of being by your side. To tell you those things would sport with your intelligence and I would not dare to do that."

"Thank—" she began in sarcasm, but he cut her off with a sharp look.

"But the moment we touched at that masquerade, you lit a fire in me. A desire to possess you that has not diminished even when I learned your true identity, even when I wanted that need to fade. When I look at you now, I see a woman I want to claim. To fuck, which is a term you will come to understand very well over the next few weeks."

She blinked. He was looking at her so intently, and there was no denying the wild, animal truth of his words. He was almost out of control, which was a state she had never seen him in, not over all the years they had known each other.

He *was* wild for her, and that made her tremble as much as his touch did, for it was unexpected and flattering and arousing beyond measure.

She swallowed, then lifted her hands. She slid her fingers beneath her chemise straps and let the scrap of silk fall away. She stood utterly naked before him and refused to be mortified in the face of his focused regard.

"Show me now what that word means," she managed to whisper past the sudden lump in her throat. "I want to know. I cannot think of anything else. It is madness and only you can end it."

"No," he said, unfastening his trousers and letting them join the pile of discarded clothing on the floor around them. His thick cock thrust against his stomach, proud and ready for the next part in their strange courtship.

"No?" she squeaked, staring at his member with wide eyes.

"No, I cannot stop the madness," he explained. "I can give you release from it momentarily, but it could take a very long time to fully clear it from your mind, from your veins, from your body."

He placed a hand on her shoulder and eased her back onto the bed. She went willingly, staring up at him as he took a place beside her. His mouth lowered and then there were no more words to be said. Only the taste of his tongue, the feel of his hands as he trailed them down the length of her body until he cupped her sex just as he had done so many times before. Her body knew what to do with that act and she arched against him in the hopes he would breech her with his talented fingers.

He did not. He merely massaged the aching entrance to her slit as he kissed and kissed and kissed her until she lost all track of time and place and consequences. He shifted until he lay over her, still kissing her. She had no feeling of fear, even when he stroked the swollen head of his member over the wet entrance to her body.

"Portia," he whispered.

She forced her eyes open and stared at him through a hooded gaze. "Yes?"

"Are you a virgin?" he asked, holding her stare with an unreadable expression.

She swallowed. Even still, he doubted her. Doubted everything she had said. But she still wanted him, wanted this. She nodded.

"I am."

He pursed his lips. "Then forgive me for this. It will be better the next time."

He fitted himself at her entrance and then slid forward, breaking the seal of her innocence in one quick movement. She gasped at the unexpected and intense pain which shot through her being. She clung to his arms, digging her nails into the flesh as her body spun with pleasure and pain, desire and fear mixed together in a confusing, intoxicating brew.

Through it all, he remained utterly still within her, watching her as she struggled with the new sensations.

"Breathe," he said softly, smoothing her hair from her forehead with the back of one hand.

She did as he suggested and sucked in a deep breath in an attempt to calm herself. As seconds passed, the pain subsided and left her with only a feeling of intimate fullness. Miles was inside her. They were one body. One being.

"Are you ready for more?" he whispered, holding her gaze evenly.

She nodded, though she didn't really know what she was saying. She wasn't prepared, she wasn't certain, she wasn't anything but filled with foggy excitement that finally she was truly wed. Finally, she was not a sad little spinster, doomed to stand in a corner for the rest of her days.

He thrust his hips in a gentle circle, and she tensed. But to her surprise, the pain she had felt at his initial breach had faded to nothingness. When he moved, there was instead a flutter of pleasure in her loins much like that when he pressed his fingers—or better yet, his tongue—inside of her.

"Do it again," she whispered, squeezing her eyes shut so she could block everything out but the sensation.

He cursed beneath his breath and thrust again. Then again. Over and over, being sure to press his pelvis to hers every single time. She arched beneath him as pain was forgotten, everything was forgotten but the heady intoxication of this act. Her body quivered as she lifted her hips to meet his,

131

her breath came in gasps and then uncontrollable sighs, and finally there was an explosion of powerful pleasure that started where their bodies met and careened through the rest of her body, filling her every nerve, cresting all the way to her fingertips as she jerked beneath him and wailed out his name again and again.

His continued to thrust through it all, though his strokes grew more erratic, harder as her crisis reached its crescendo. Suddenly he groaned loudly and she felt his seed spill hot within her clenching body.

For a long moment, he remained there, his forehead pressed to hers and his body still joined with hers. But then he flopped back against the coverlet beside her, panting as their bodies parted. She lay there, staring at the ceiling and simply enjoying the tingling aftermath of what he had done to her.

She looked at him from the corner of her eye and immediately the desire he had quenched with his skilled seduction began to build again.

"You were right," she whispered, shaking at the boldness of what she was about to say.

"Right?" he asked, his own breath short as he rolled on his side to look down at her in the firelight.

"You told me earlier that you could ease the madness of my desire, but not quench it entirely." She smiled at him. "I want more, Miles. I want to do it all again."

Chapter Twelve

Miles stared down at Portia, her eyes still wide and innocent, her words most definitely not so. She had been untouched, just as she had claimed. He knew that to be true, for he had felt her body give when he slid home inside of her, he had seen evidence of her pain both in her reaction and the light staining of blood on his sheets.

Still, she was so responsive, so open to sin and seduction...he had to wonder if he *was* the first man to have pleasured her in some way, even if she had never been penetrated.

Yet even with those questions in his mind, her words, her demand rang in his ears and made his body stir.

"You must give me time to recover," he said as he stroked his fingers between her breasts. She sighed at the touch, shutting her eyes as he traced the smooth lines of her flesh gently.

"How long?" she asked without looking at him.

"Demanding little minx," he chuckled. "Not very if you keep up this line of questioning."

"Good." She snuggled closer and rested her head on the crook of his shoulder. "While we wait, perhaps we could talk about something."

He tensed. How many lovers had wished to talk after making love? It had never been something he looked forward to.

"What do you wish to discuss?" he asked, caution in every word.

She kept her eyes shut, though blood pinkened her cheeks ever so slightly. "Our—our bargain, my lord. I made you an offer and now that you have claimed me, I would like to know what it entails."

He cleared his throat. Now *this* was a topic he could embrace, if only to see what her reaction would be to his shocking responses.

"I think it is a fair question, my dear," he said. "And now that you have been, as you say, *claimed*, it does seem as good a time as any to open the floor to it."

Finally she looked at him through hooded lids and said, "You said you would introduce me to pleasures I had never imagined. That you would take me beyond my boundaries. What will that entail?"

He cleared his throat. "Portia, when you went to the masquerade, you saw what people did there. Out in the open for everyone to see, they played in pleasure."

She nodded, a jerky motion.

"They do it because some people like to *be* watched while they share their bodies. Others go there because they like *to* watch." He cupped one breasts absently, strumming her hard nipple with his thumb. "Did you like to watch them?"

She hesitated, and he gave her a stern gaze.

"No lies now, Portia. I won't judge you."

"I-I did feel arousal while watching them copulate." She arched as he touched her, her breath coming short as her body reacted to him and to what they were discussing. Most interesting, indeed. "And now that you and I have...now that I understand more fully, remembering that night makes me—"

She cut herself off and he chuckled. "Wet?"

Her face jerked to him. "Is that normal?"

He smiled. The more she talked, the more innocent she seemed, and it was confusing and amazing and arousing all at once.

"It is exactly what you want. The slickness your body creates makes my entering you more comfortable and pleasurable for us both," he assured her. He lowered his hand between her legs to press his fingertips inside of her. "And making you wet is certainly a great pleasure."

She whimpered, twisting to get closer, and he withdrew his fingers.

"We won't get anything done this way." He laughed.

She struggled to regain her composure and then sucked in a harsh breath. "And what of you, Miles. Do *you* like to watch?"

He nodded without hesitation. "I like to watch and sometimes to be watched by others. And the idea of being caught can be quite arousing, as well, when it comes to pleasuring in public arenas. You recall our encounter in my office earlier today."

"Anyone could have come in," she said.

"That's the fun of it," he replied. Now his body was stirring after the satisfied slumber of release. His cock began to ache.

"So you will have me be a part of those desires?" she asked.

He nodded. "I would very much like to see you become aroused by watching others. I want you to watch others even while you, yourself, are touched and pleasured."

She considered that a moment. "Will it be known that it is me?"

He shrugged. "Your face would be covered, but I'm sure some will guess. Now that you are married, it will be less talk, for anyone there is also participating in something they would not want the world at large to know about, either."

"Funny that my innocence condemned me more than my true wickedness will," she mused.

"That is the way of the world, I fear," he said.

She stared up at him. "Will I be...will I be safe?"

He drew back. "Yes. Always. I would never leave your side or expose you to anyone who might wish to harm you."

An uncertain expression remained on her face, and he frowned.

"You can depend on me, Portia. You will come to realize that."

She was silent for a moment, but then her hand lifted and she wound her fingers into his hair and drew his lips to hers. He claimed them eagerly, sucking her tongue gently as he rolled to cover her a second time. His cock was hard, having swollen and readied during their talk, and he gently breeched her, taking care because she was probably still sore from their first joining.

She was like heaven around him, hot and tight, squeezing him with internal muscles like a natural wanton would do. He rocked into her, reveling in how she lifted her hips to meet him while moans and mewls of pleasure left her lips with every thrust.

He kept up those steady, gentle strokes for a long time, until he lost track of the count of them, until her breath caught and her nails dug into his shoulders. Beneath him, she began to shake, biting her lip and gasping as her crisis built. Finally, she let out a cry and her body convulsed beneath him, shaking as she came.

Her reaction, so real and so genuine, drove him over the edge, and for the second time he let loose his seed inside of her, crying out her name as he pounded the last of his pleasure into her arching body.

She wrapped her arms around him tightly as he fell against her body, his breath short and his heart pounding. Gently, she smoothed her fingers down his spine.

He relaxed against the unexpectedly tender touch. Women in his life always knew their place. They were lovers—they didn't expect to last longer than a night. Even his mistresses had always accepted the boundaries he placed upon them. He liked sex and that was all he required from any female who shared his bed.

So it had been a very long time since someone offered more. Offered...this.

He extracted himself from her arms gently and rolled to lie beside her on the bed. She shot him a side-glance but did not follow or demand anything more.

"Sleep now," he said, trying to soften the distance he had just placed between them. "You have earned the rest."

Her lips parted, almost as if she wanted to say something else to him, but stopped herself. Then she slowly rolled to her side facing away from him and closed her eyes.

He watched her for a long time. He watched her breathing slow and become more even, he watched her relax into slumber and even knew when she began to dream as her hands clenched and she murmured incoherent words in her sleep.

But it wasn't the words she whispered that he wondered about. It was what she was going to say before she rolled away that haunted him. And it was the thought that maybe, just maybe, she had thought of another man all day. Or that she wished she was in someone else's bed.

"It doesn't bloody matter," he said with a shake of his head as he flopped a forearm over his eyes and tried to force sleep upon himself. "If she doesn't care for you any deeper than a friendship, any deeper than desire, it is all the better for her. For you."

But as he slipped into his own dreamless slumber, a piercing thought intruded. There was a screaming voice he couldn't silence that told him he was wrong. That maybe, for once in his life, he *should* want more. That maybe, for the first time ever, he could have more.

Portia's eyes fluttered open, and she looked around the chamber in a moment of confusion. This wasn't her tiny room with its rickety furniture and lumpy bed that made her back ache. This was...

Then her mind cleared. This was Miles' house. This was her husband's bed, where she had spent her wedding night exploring pleasure and discussing a shocking future she could scarce imagine.

She rolled onto her back, lifting the sheet to cover her bare breasts. She was alone, though the rumpled sheets spoke of Miles being there with her through the night. That and a neatly folded note resting there with her name scrawled across the face.

She plucked it from its place and sat up. Before she read it, she shook her head. How had she not heard him get up? Normally, she was on pins and needles all night long. The slightest blowing of the breeze would wake her. But here...she had apparently slept like the dead.

With a sigh, she opened the note and read, "When you wake, ring and someone will help you ready yourself. If I am not in the dining room, please find me in my office. M."

The words weren't exactly romantic, but they weren't cold either. They were simply there, a deeper meaning unreadable, just as everything was with Miles. He showed her a surface self, but nothing more.

"Do I want more?" she muttered as she got out of bed.

Her clothing was gone. Another piece of evidence that she had slept very well, indeed, but a robe had been left draped across the chair for her. She pulled it on and rang for a servant.

Almost immediately, a girl arrived with a smile.

"Good morning, Lady Weatherfield," she said, cheery as she entered the room.

"Oh my," Portia said with a shake of her head. "That is me, isn't it?"

The young woman laughed. "Indeed. You'll get used to it soon enough. My name is Bridget and I'm a maid for the house, but I'll serve as your lady's maid until you choose another. Why don't we go into your chamber?"

Portia blinked but followed the girl slowly. Now that it was daylight, she could finally see the bedroom that would be called hers. As she passed through the door, she caught her breath.

It was beautiful. It was three times as big as her chamber in the house her brother provided, with a massive cherry wood wardrobe and a matching dressing table. A full-length mirror sat in one corner. The walls had been painted a soft, rabbit-fur gray with white and slight rose accents throughout the fine paintings and other décor.

Portia swayed on her feet and only just caught the back of the chair beside the dressing table to steady herself. Immediately Bridget was at her side, her eyes wide.

"Oh, my lady, are you well?"

Portia blushed. "Yes, I am fine, I'm sorry. It's only—" Tears stung her eyes and she covered her mouth to keep a sob in. "I'm sorry, it's been so long since I've had such a fine room. Since I've had anything that was just...*mine.*"

The maid's expression softened. "Well, you have that and more here, my lady," she said quietly as she produced a handkerchief seemingly from nowhere. "And his lordship has already declared that you should change anything you like in this room to personalize it."

Portia shook her head. "I wouldn't change a thing," she whispered.

Bridget chose not to answer and instead turned toward the wardrobe. "Let me select one of your pretty new gowns and we can have you ready in a moment."

Portia smiled as the girl opened the wardrobe and began to flick through the small collection of gowns. She was very good. The very best servants knew when to be kind, but also when to give an employer his or her space to compose themselves.

Which Portia did before the young woman turned back, holding up a new dress. It was a lovely pale green with fine hand-stitched accents.

"This one will be very pretty with your hair," Bridget suggested.

Portia nodded. "Very well."

In a moment, the maid had stripped her from the silken robe and began to help her into the dress.

"His lordship said to let you have your breakfast, but if you'd like a bath after, we can begin to prepare one." Bridget cast her eyes down. "It may...help."

Portia blushed, but what was there to be said? The previous night being her wedding night—the entire household knew what she had been doing.

"Thank you, that would be lovely," Portia said, then hastened to change the embarrassing subject. "How long have you worked here?"

Bridget smiled as she fastened buttons and smoothed silk carefully. "Oh goodness, near five years now. My mama was once a maid here. When she died, I was offered a place by Lord Weatherfield himself."

Portia shook her head. The girl couldn't be more than twenty-one. To lose her mother so young hurt Portia to her soul.

"That was kind," she replied when it was clear Bridget expected a response.

"Oh yes, very kind. But he is the very best of masters, as any of the servants will tell you. Never sharp and always willing to help. He is generous in his wagers and the days we have to ourselves."

Portia sucked in the new information like a greedy sponge. She knew full well that a man could easily be measured by his treatment of his servants. Her father and her brother were both terrible to theirs. That Miles was respected and even liked by those in his employ spoke highly of him.

"And what of the house?" Portia pressed. "Is there anything I should know as I embark upon my new life here?"

Bridget finished with the gown and motioned for Portia to sit at the dressing table where she began to brush her tangled blond hair.

"Let me think. There is a glorious library downstairs that Lord Weatherfield encourages everyone in the house to enjoy freely. And a music room where Lady Tennille..." The girl blushed. "I'm sorry, Lady Brinforth, once practiced her pianoforte daily. She is a talented musician."

Portia bit her lip. Although it was expected for ladies of her station to be proficient in some kind of art, she had never been encouraged to play or sing or sew or anything else. Either money or mocking had kept her from pursuing those things.

"I cannot wait to have the pleasure of hearing her play," Portia finally said with an only slightly forced smile.

"Oh and the garden is most beautiful," Bridget added as she pressed a final pin into Portia's locks and smiled at the reflection. "There, you look lovely, my lady. I'm sure your husband and your mother will be enchanted."

Portia jolted a little at the statement and stared up at the maid. "My—my mother?"

The girl seemed to sense her surprise and shifted uncomfortably. "Yes. They are having a meal together in the breakfast room that faces the east."

Portia swallowed, trying not to think of how that was going. "How long have they been together?"

Bridget shook her head. "Half an hour, perhaps?"

Portia pushed to her feet. "Show me to the breakfast room, Bridget. Hurry!"

Chapter Thirteen

Miles smiled as he passed a plate of toast down the table to his mother-in-law. Instead of taking the topmost piece, she took the second one down, then buttered it as she continued talking.

"My husband was just the same way, I fear. Stuck on the idea of catching some ridiculously large fish from that pond. I told him again and again that there were only minnows in the water, but he never believed me."

She laughed and Miles laughed with her, stricken by how funny and aware she could be. He had seen her detached and broken before. His heart hurt for Portia. In some ways, these times of lucidity had to make the longer stretches of madness all the more difficult.

"I imagine all men are driven to catch the biggest fish," he said as he smiled at her. "It is in our nature, you cannot change it."

Portia's mother's laughter faded a bit. "But sometimes it is better to be satisfied with the fish we have caught. Otherwise, you will never get to supper at all."

Miles arched a brow at her words and her rather sharp expression. It seemed her ladyship was making a point, and it wasn't a bad one. Apparently his reputation preceded him, even with a mother-in-law who had been shut in for years. He would have to tread very carefully here if he didn't want to bring himself grief or cause Lady Cosslow any pain or confusion.

But before he could respond at all, the door to the breakfast room flew open and Portia was revealed in the entryway, her eyes wide and her face pink with both exertion and emotion. She stared, first at her mother, then to him, then back to Lady Cosslow a second time. Her panic was obvious and it cut him to the bone.

"Portia," he drawled, rising to his feet. "How lovely to see you this morning—did you sleep well?"

She looked at him as if she didn't understand the question and then her focus drifted back to her mother. "I—"

Lady Cosslow didn't seem to be aware at all of her daughter's distress. "Portia, darling. I was just breaking my fast with your husband. Will you not join us?"

Portia drew in a few long breaths and then moved toward them with slow uncertainty. "Mama, how are you feeling?"

Her mother blinked. "Why, I am very well."

"I see." Portia swallowed and her disbelief and wariness was lined across her face.

How many times had she had this conversation with her mother? How many times had it deteriorated into something terrible?

"Please, Portia, join us," Miles said, coming around the table to take her hand. The second their skin touched, he was jolted by desire and keen awareness of her scent, her warmth, her being in general.

She seemed just as moved, if the slight increase in her breathing was any indication. Her fingers trembled ever so slightly, but she didn't pull away and allowed him to take her to the table and help her settle into a place across from her mother and beside him.

He motioned to a footman waiting at the door. Immediately the young man stepped to his side.

"Portia, how would you like to break your fast?" he asked softly.

She shook her head. "I don't know. I don't usually—" She cut herself off with a furious blush and Miles' heart almost stopped.

She didn't eat breakfast...because her brother hadn't provided her with enough funds to afford it. He had never wanted to pummel a man so much in his life. But he remained calm.

"Bring her ladyship some tea, eggs, bacon and toast. Oh, and be sure Mrs. Flynn puts her homemade jam on the tray."

The young man bobbed his head at the order and slipped silently from the room. Portia said nothing, but stared at Miles, eyes wide.

He ignored the expression and instead smiled at her. "Once you have eaten, I would greatly like to take you on a tour of the London house. We will stay in Town until the weather improves, so I want you to be comfortable here."

"Yes," Portia nodded, and her voice sounded a little more normal now that they were having a rational conversation and she wasn't having to defend her mother or herself. "I would like that."

"Lady Cosslow, you should join us in that tour," Miles added, extending his smile to his new mother-in-law.

Lady Cosslow blinked at him, as confused by this request as Portia seemed to be by finding them breaking bread together a few moments before.

"I would be in the way," Lady Cosslow said softly.

Once again, Miles saw his mother-in-law's awareness of her limitations and his heart ached for that pain she tried to hide.

"Nonsense, you wouldn't be in the way in the slightest. After all, you will be living here, as well." Miles touched her hand briefly. "I would like for you to come."

Slowly, Lady Cosslow cast a glance to her daughter and when she found Portia smiling at her, she nodded. "If you would like me to join you, I wouldn't be so rude as to deny you. I look forward to seeing this beautiful home more thoroughly."

"Then it is settled," Miles said as the servant placed a plate before Portia. "When you are finished, we shall begin."

She nodded and began to eat, but Portia never took her eyes from his face. And though he shifted beneath her close regard, he couldn't help but feel that this brief moment where someone saw him as a hero was a feeling he could grow accustomed to.

If only he weren't such a rake.

Portia trailed a few steps behind her new husband and her mother as Miles led them on a tour of his home. She couldn't help but ponder how very different the man was than he had ever led anyone to believe. A rogue, a rake, even a cad were words she had sometimes heard used about him...but he was nothing of the sort.

He was intelligent, he was amusing, and he was kind...so very kind to her mother that she almost couldn't bear it, for no one had been kind to Thomasina in years.

Even now, her mother had her arm linked through his and was chatting and laughing with him as if the world was a normal place for her. It was only the occasional twitch of her eyes or hesitation in her step that would let anyone know that her mother wasn't well. She had even done reasonably well when they all met the servants, though her mother had taken Portia's hand and clung to it rather than saying hello.

Portia smiled, tugging herself from her musings. "You have taken us all over this beautiful house, Miles, but you have not shown us the one place that intrigues me most."

He cast a quick glance over his shoulder at her and their eyes met briefly. He had mischief in his eyes, mixed with a flash of powerful desire that hit her low in the gut and made her ache with her own mirrored need.

How could he do such things to her with just a heated glance?

"And what have I withheld?" he teased. "I would not wish to leave you *unsatisfied*."

Portia swallowed hard at his choice of words. "Why, your library, my lord," she managed to squeeze out past a tight throat.

He arched a brow and then nodded. "Of course! But I have not forgotten, I merely saved the best for last."

He pointed to a set of large double doors at the end of one of the twisting hallways they had come by. He released her mother's hand and moved to them. Before he opened them, though, he turned back.

"My library is open to all who live in this house. I hope you will take full advantage."

Then he smiled, an expression filled with pride and boyish glee at what he would reveal. His excitement was catching, for Portia's heart lodged in her throat as the doors opened and revealed the most magnificent thing she had ever seen.

The room was massive, twice the size of his splendid ballroom where they had taken their vows, with vaulted ceilings at least two stories above where they stood capped with a glass dome that allowed natural light to merge with that of the lamps and fire.

The fireplace was a giant thing with a mantel of rock and decorated brass that reflected columns of gold along the bookshelves that lined every wall.

They were so high that there were ladders all around the room to reach the upper reaches of the shelves.

"Great...God," Portia breathed, stepping in beside him to stare.

"Close your mouth, wife," he said close to her ear, mimicking his words from the night before when she first saw him naked.

She was nearly as impressed now as she had been then, but she smiled up at him at their shared reference. He stared at her a long moment, his gaze hooded and unreadable, before he turned to her mother.

"Lady Cosslow, won't you excuse us a moment?"

Her mother nodded. "I will take the opportunity to greedily peruse your shelves."

He smiled, caught Portia by her elbow and dragged her out of the library, down the hall and into a small parlor nearby. He hauled her inside, slammed the door and suddenly he was pressing her against the barrier, his mouth hot and hard against hers as he dragged his tongue against hers.

She gasped for breath as he pulled away and gave her a sliver of space between them. *There* was the rake, the rogue, the seducer he had been hiding. But the curtain had been pulled back and now she saw him as more.

"What is that appraising look," he asked, wiping his mouth. "Are you judging my techniques already?"

She laughed softly. "No, I am simply thinking about what a charlatan you are."

His eyes grew wide. "A shocking accusation, indeed. And very serious." He paced away. "But I have no idea what you could mean."

"Don't you?" Portia asked, folding her arms as she watched him shuffle in discomfort. "You are known as a cad. In fact, you seem to revel in your bad reputation...but you are not at all what you pretend to be."

He stared at her. "What am I, Portia?"

"You are a good man, with far more depth than you allow anyone to see." She motioned to the door behind her. "Anyone with eyes could determine how proud you are of your library, how eager you are to share it. That is not the hobby of a libertine. And your kindness toward me, toward my mother, under the worst of circumstances—" She caught her breath. "Well, not even my own brother can manage a fraction of your goodness when it comes to her."

He stared at her for a long moment and then he moved on her. He pushed her against the door a second time, pinning her with a hand on either side of her head, his face close to hers.

"Portia, I'm leaving for a while, going out to take care of a bit of business that cannot be avoided," he said, his sweet breath warm on her face. "But I would suggest you take your bath and ready yourself while I am gone, for when I come home, I will not be good. I will not be nice. I will prove to you that whatever you think you know about me after just a few days of being close, I live up to my wicked reputation perfectly well."

Her breath caught as she stared up at his handsome face. "Is that meant to be a threat?"

He smiled, but there was darkness and sensuality in that expression. "A promise, my dear."

Boldness like she'd never known filled her, and she lifted up on her tiptoes, winding her arms around his neck to brush her lips back and forth against his. He allowed her the teasing

149

for a moment, before he cupped the back of her head and kissed her far more properly. His tongue tangled with hers, sucking her in, making her weak and needy before he released her and stepped back, panting.

"I-I certainly look forward to whatever you will do when you return," Portia said with an incline of her head.

He stared at her for a moment, reached around her to open the door. She stepped away and allowed him to walk through it. He turned back.

"Be ready."

Then he left her standing in the parlor, gaping after him and filled with a combination of nervousness and desperate anticipation that would not be eased until the next time he touched her.

Portia walked back into the library and smiled when she found her mother tucked up in a comfortable settee, a book on her lap and four others in a pile next to her.

"Goodness, you do make yourself at home," she laughed.

Her mother glanced up with a smile. "Your new husband is quite a man."

Portia stiffened. "He is indeed."

"You never told me how it was that you two courted and became engaged." Her mother set her book aside and looked up at her. "You...you did not hide it from me, did you?"

Portia rushed to sit next to her. "No! No, I promise you, Mama. It is...complicated. Our engagement was very sudden."

Her mother's lips pursed together. "I realize that I have not done for you what a mother should."

Portia took her hand. "Mama..."

Thomasina shrugged. "There is no use denying it. I try so very hard to stay in this place, to understand what is happening around me, but when the darkness comes...when I am overtaken, I cannot stop it, no matter how I try. And you have suffered for it, probably the greatest of all."

Swallowing hard, Portia squeezed her mother's hands. "I know if you could change it, you would."

"And my problems have certainly kept me from talking to you about what to expect from a husband, from a marriage."

"I don't think anyone ever believed I would need that advice," Portia said, her tone witheringly dry. "I was an old maid until—"

Her mother stared at her, focused, of course, in this moment where Portia would have preferred a little lack of understanding.

"Until what?"

She cleared her throat. "We were caught in a compromising position, Mama. Very compromising. He never would have thought twice about marrying me unless we had been," she admitted with a blush.

Her tone sounded so harsh, she hadn't fully realized just how bitter that truth made her.

Her mother frowned. "I'm sorry to hear that, my dear. I wanted more for you than a marriage not of your choosing. It is what I got and as you know, your father and I were desperately unhappy together."

Portia nodded. She had seen her parents, two utterly different people, grow to resent each other. And the more troubled her mother had become, the more her father's resentment turned to utter hatred. He had poisoned her brother with that sentiment. He had poisoned everything around them.

"I don't want my life to take that turn," she whispered, thinking of Miles and his expression when he'd realized the woman behind the mask was *her*.

He had been horrified. And though they had connected since then, she knew that horror was still there. That at any moment, he could go back to feeling disgusted by her and her treachery. Then his kiss, his touch, his desire and even his kindness could be snatched away forever.

She blinked away those troubling thoughts.

"Miles seems a better sort than your father," her mother reassured her gently. "But, Portia, you must do your part to develop a relationship with him. To make your marriage as real as he will allow, even if it wasn't one of his asking."

Portia blushed as she thought of the bargain she had made with Miles on her mother's behalf. Of the way he had claimed her the night before and promised her wicked pleasures to come.

Their marriage certainly felt real at the moment.

But desire would fade. He would bore of her and her mother was correct. If she didn't want Miles' resentment, she would have to find a way to have a relationship with him outside of his bed.

To her surprise, that task seemed almost as daunting as the bargain she had made with her body. With Miles, it seemed, she was forever on shifting sands. And she wasn't certain she would ever be entirely confident about where she stood.

Chapter Fourteen

He never should have come here.

Miles stood and paced around the parlor. This was a terrible mistake and he knew it. But could he escape the trap he had set for himself?

He moved for the door, but just as he reached it, it opened and his sister stepped inside. She jumped as she saw how close he was.

"Gracious, Miles, no need to stand in wait." She laughed as she motioned him back to his seat and poured him a cup of tea. "Granger must have told you I was coming presently."

"He did." Miles sighed as he took the cup and set it aside. "I only thought of another appointment I had forgotten."

His sister's smile faded ever so slightly and she folded her hands.

"Out with it. What is it?" she asked.

He cleared his throat in discomfort. "What is what?"

"I know you better than anyone in this world," Tennille said softly. "And I know when you are troubled. Which is, I suppose, why you have shown up on my doorstep, unannounced, one day after your wedding, when you should be at home with your new bride. So tell me, what is it? Are things not going well between you and Portia already?"

Miles shoved to his feet and walked to the window. "Of course they are going well," he reassured her and thought of Portia's sweet surrender in his bed the night before. "Portia is...unexpected."

"Good," his sister laughed. "You need a woman who will confuse you."

"Thank you so very much," he said, tone dry though he smiled. "I prefer to say she challenges me."

"Fine, argue the semantics. *But?*" his sister encouraged.

He thought for a moment, thought of everything he had come to know about Portia. Everything she had been through, everything she had suffered. And how she had handled those terrible things.

"I have come to the decision that I need to spoil my wife," he said.

His sister speared him with an appraising glance, then swallowed her sip of tea with a nod. "Good. She deserves it, poor girl."

Miles pursed his lips. He didn't particularly like the fact that Tennille *pitied* Portia. Although, to be fair, he had bestowed his own pity upon her more than once over the years. But that was before he knew her. Now he recognized that she was not pitiable at all, but rather *admirable*. She had a deep well of inner strength one would never guess when watching her hug a wall with the other spinsters.

That inner strength intrigued him beyond measure, for he had always gauged that he possessed it himself, as did his sister.

"The problem is that I do not exactly know how to go about that sort of thing when it comes to a wife," he admitted. "And you are the only wife I know who I trust to talk to about such a delicate subject. So how in the world do I go about indulging her?"

Tennille shook her head. "You act as though you are deciphering an impossible puzzle."

He scrubbed a hand over his face. "It feels as though I am."

She sighed. "For God's sake, Miles, she is a person, not a quandary. Get to know her. Discover her little hopes and forgotten dreams. If you can manage it, return those things to her. Anticipate her desires before she even knows she has them. Of course, this will require intense focus on her."

Miles swallowed hard as, once again, he was bombarded with images of Portia arching beneath him. Portia crying out his name as he pleasured her. If he could anticipate those physical desires, was it so much of a stretch to try to guess any others she might have?

"We are newly married—I think intense focus on her is what is required, is it not?" he asked, trying to keep his wicked thoughts from being too obvious.

Tennille frowned. "Of course, I must warn you that there could be a side effect to this experiment of yours."

"A side effect?"

"Yes. Portia just might fall in love with you." His sister folded her arms as she awaited his response to that statement.

His stomach turned at the thought and he shook his head. "That would be a great mistake on her part."

His sister moved closer. "I beg to differ, Miles," she whispered. "I think it would be a wonderful thing...for both of you. You deserve someone to love you. Your fear of that is—"

He turned away. "Hush," he interrupted. "Enough of this."

But she ignored his sharp order. "No, I will not hush. We *never* speak of the past."

He flinched. Pain he kept at bay with great effort began to seep into his body, into his soul.

"For good reason," he choked out.

"The abuse we suffered as children was unfair," his sister continued despite his admonishments. "You tried to protect me,

155

which is proof of the goodness inside of you. It is proof that you are capable of great things, of great love."

He shook his head. "I do not want to be capable of that."

Tennille let out a little sob that forced him to look at her. Her eyes were filled with tears and she had her arms folded. She looked so very, very sad. So pitying of him. It cut him to his heart.

"I know firsthand how healing love can be," she whispered when she had regained some measure of composure. "Like you, I fought it at every turn, but it came anyway, and it was so worth the sacrifices and the vulnerability I had to have to earn it."

Miles stared at her. He had been involved in all his sister's Seasons, of course. He had provided her with all she needed for great success and he had been pleased at her choice of Richard. The viscount was a decent man.

More importantly, Miles had seen their affection, their love for one another. But never once had he considered that their relationship might have been difficult for Tennille to accept.

That she would be as haunted by the past, by the demons of their childhood, as he was.

"I'm glad for you," he said, taking her hand in his and squeezing it. "I love that you are happy, that you are loved and that you are capable of giving love in return. You deserve that and so much more."

She smiled. "And so do you. So if love comes calling, I hope you will not turn it away out of hand. At least consider giving your marriage, your wife, your *heart* a chance at something deeper than a mere façade of a union."

Miles swallowed his retort. There was nothing he could say that would change his sister's view on his life or his relationship. But she was wrong. He was capable of a great deal, but fully opening himself to love?

That was impossible.

He had seen what love could do, how it could destroy. His best option was to stay far clear of it. And to make sure Portia didn't do anything so foolish as convince herself that she loved him.

It was the best gift he could bestow. For both of them.

Portia was in her chamber, going through her dolefully small collection of things that had been brought from the house her brother let.

"Honestly," she muttered as she lifted a worn chemise to the light and shook her head. "We lived as paupers."

She tensed and set the item aside when she heard the carriage pull into the drive. She moved to the window and looked down as Miles stepped from the vehicle and spoke for a moment to the servant who greeted him.

Even from far above, his confidence was clear. The way he stood, the way he tilted his head as he listened, the way he clapped the other man on the back before he moved toward the house, they all spoke of his utter surety in himself.

But then, men like Miles were golden in their Society. Men with money and property, with history to their names and a tiny hint of scandal on their backs were practically worshipped. Certainly she would be hated by all the women who had once pursued him the next time she entered a ballroom on his arm.

She was not looking forward to that moment, nor to the Season to come when their scandal would be whispered about amongst all who had not been in Town over the winter.

"Preserve us," she muttered as she returned her attention to her things.

She had two piles at present. Things to dispose of and things to keep. The disposal pile was far higher and consisted mostly of a few overly patched gowns and worn slippers. She was almost embarrassed to give them over to Bridget, who was still serving as her lady's maid until the time when she could interview the others Armstrong had apparently arranged for her to meet.

Another item on the growing list of things the new Lady Weatherfield would be expected to do.

"Being a lady is quite tedious, it seems," she said to herself.

"Then don't be one," said a voice from her door.

She blushed as she turned to find Miles there. She glanced at the window.

"Did you come straight up to me?" she asked.

His brow wrinkled. "You knew I was home?"

"I saw you on the drive," she admitted and wondered what he thought of her spying. Why could she not *think* before she spoke to this man?

He blinked, but offered no other reaction to that admission.

"I did come straight up to you, my lady," he said with a shrug, as he came into her room and closed the door behind himself. "I did not expect you to be here lamenting your position in life."

"I wasn't," she hastened to say. "I am greatly appreciative of all you have—"

"Oh, please," he groaned, tossing her careful pile of clothing to discard on the floor and flopping down on his stomach on the bed. "Spare me more grateful speeches. I didn't *give* you anything, Portia. We found ourselves in a situation we are now both making the best of. You owe me no more than I owe you."

158

"That isn't true and you know it," Portia said with a shake of her head. "You could have turned your back on me, refused to make me your bride, and I would have been destroyed in Society."

He arched a brow. "You think my own consequences wouldn't have been as dire? To compromise a lady and then not do the right thing?"

"Don't be thick, it doesn't suit you," Portia sighed. "I was nothing more than a spinster no one else wanted and you are golden as a god. If you had refused me, yes, this Season would have been uncomfortable for you, and I'm certain there would be a few families who would no longer consider you for their daughters. But you are highly liked, Miles. And your title and your money wouldn't have changed just because you set aside an utterly undesirable girl. After a year, everyone would have conveniently forgotten what you did and you would have been as sought out as ever."

He stared at her, as if her words were foreign. As if he had never considered that possibility.

"Think of Lord Yeardley," she said softly. "He ruined Isabel Krispen three years ago. She is in exile still, with a bastard child no less. He and his new wife, the one with the money and the good family, are still invited to *every* soiree of importance."

He nodded. "Yes, you are correct. It is beastly. But I am not half the ass that Yeardley is, I hope you will grant me that."

She stared at him, with his crooked smile and true regret in his eyes. It was almost as if he...understood her. Or at the very least, he truly listened to her. When was the last time that had happened outside of Ava?

"Yeardley isn't fit to shine your shoes," she said with a brief smile.

Their eyes met, and suddenly the mood in the room changed. She felt the desire in Miles grow and her own body answered those unspoken cues as they stared at each other.

Then he shook his head and rolled from the bed to stand up again.

"So what duties of a lady were you lamenting, exactly, when I came in?"

She shrugged. It seemed mundane to discuss these silly household matters with him, but since he had asked…

"Armstrong has a bevy of lady's maid candidates for me to interview this week, but I admit I do not relish the task. I feel foolish doing it."

"You shouldn't," he said with a shake of his head.

"Shouldn't, but do," she replied with a laugh she hoped sounded light. "I'm terribly out of practice with my 'lady of the house' routine. To be honest, I was never much good at it to begin with."

He smiled. "Then what would make it easier?"

She drew back. "I'm sorry?"

"What would take the burden away?" he said. "Certainly there must be an alternative."

"Well…I-I like Bridget, the maid who has been helping me. She is efficient, kind and very good at the role. I connected with her almost upon the first moment we met," she admitted.

She waited for him to refuse her, to say she was foolish or to claim that Bridget was needed elsewhere in the house.

Instead, he shrugged. "Then tell Armstrong. Trust me, the man may look imposing, but he is a lamb on the inside. If you tell him you would like to commandeer Bridget for the task, he will grant that to you without hesitation, I'm certain."

She swallowed. "Could *you* tell him?"

He stared at her for a long moment before he answered, "No. You will have to be able to manage the servants, my dear. You know that. But I will tell you what—I'll go with you when you inform him."

She bit her lip. That would do, for he was right that if she was to be mistress of this house, she couldn't avoid managing it.

"Now?" she asked.

But he wasn't watching her anymore. He was looking at her mouth. Staring at it and his eyes were lit with even more desire.

"Not now," he said, moving on her. "Right now I plan to strip you out of those clothes and have my wicked way with you."

Her eyes went wide as he reached out and caught her waist. He tugged her against him and pressed his mouth to hers. The chemise still in her hands fluttered to the ground between them and she wound her arms around his neck, opening her mouth to him and swirling her tongue against his in surrender.

He groaned, the sound reverberating through her body until the echoes of it settled between her legs. She arched, almost against her will, rubbing her pelvis against his and feeling the hard evidence that he desired her still.

But she couldn't stop to wonder at that fact. He pushed her against the bed roughly and began to unfasten her buttons along the front of her gown. She lifted her hands to his shirt, and together they raced to undress the other.

When his shirt parted to reveal that beautiful, male torso, she couldn't help herself. She leaned forward to press a kiss against his taut stomach.

He jerked at the contact of her lips to his flesh.

"I'm sorry," she whispered, blushing. "Is that wrong?"

"Far from it," he panted. "But you shall steal my control if you continue that."

She arched a brow at the thought. "I've never stolen a man's control before," she murmured.

He shook his head. "That is because men are idiots. I include myself, because had I known what a pleasure you would be, I would have ruined you, married you and bedded you years ago. Though perhaps I would have altered the order a fraction, for the sake of our reputations."

She swallowed. No man had ever looked at her like this. No man had ever spoken to her like this. And she drank it up like a plant deprived of water in the desert.

"Then it seems, my lord, that you should make up for lost time."

He didn't respond with words but by drawing her gaping dress open and dragging a hand between her breasts through her chemise.

"I agree," he grunted and pulled the dress away entirely. The chemise swiftly followed and he was on her again, kissing her, rubbing against her, lifting her breasts before he lowered his mouth from hers and began to suckle her nipples, one after another.

Pleasure ripped through her with almost violent power, forcing her to moan with incoherent madness as she opened her legs, lifted her back, offered herself like a lightskirt.

He pressed a hand between her legs as he continued to swirl his tongue around the sensitive nipple and pressed the tips of two fingers inside of her clenching sheath.

"My God, the things you do to me," he panted as he drew back. "Roll over."

She stared at him, uncomprehending, which must have been reflected on her face, for he smiled. Her heart caught at that wicked, knowing expression.

"You told me you would surrender completely. So trust that I will take care of you. You will like this."

She bit back any nervous words and slowly rolled onto her stomach. He placed his hands beneath her hips and lifted them, putting her on display. Blood rushed to her cheeks as she buried her head in the pillow, but she still felt his heated stare burning into the bare flesh of her backside.

She was utterly exposed in this position, completely vulnerable to whatever he decided to do.

His choice was as shocking as his demand, for suddenly his hands were on her thighs, spreading her wider before his hot breath stirred against the entrance to her sex. As she gasped with surprise, he stroked his tongue along her slit and she bucked with pleasure.

He gripped her hips, drawing her against his mouth, delving his tongue deep inside her channel, flicking it against her clitoris as he rocked her back against his lips.

She gripped the coverlet with both hands, scraping her nails against the fabric as pleasure spiraled out of control from the point where he touched her and spread throughout every nerve of her body. She bit her lip to keep her cries inside, but he pressed on, tormenting her with his tongue while he released her hip with one hand and slipped two fingers deep within her pussy.

He pulled back. "Moan for me," he ordered.

She bit out a broken sound of pleasure.

"Yes," he whispered, his voice strained. "Now touch yourself while I make you come."

Her eyes flew open and she stared at the wall in surprise as he returned his mouth to her tingling sex. Touch herself. While he did this. It was so wicked, so wild, so intimate and yet she had promised him she would acquiesce to his every demand.

Slowly, she let her fingers thread through the soft curls between her legs. They settled against the bundle of nerves hidden within, and she jolted at the pressure, the pleasure.

"That's right," he murmured against her flesh. "Feel how wet you are from my lips, from your own excitement, how hot and ready you are for my cock. Help me bring you pleasure before I take you."

She shuddered at his sinful words. A lady was not supposed to like such things, and yet her clitoris throbbed madly at his low tone. She began to stroke herself gently, thrusting back against his lips as pleasure washed over her in wild, confusing waves.

Everything about her became focused on her sex, on the pressure of his fingers, of her own fingers, of his tongue, of his breath. And then orgasm overtook her. She screamed as her hips flailed wildly against his mouth, but before her release was complete, his touch was gone.

She peeked over her shoulder and found he had sat up, lips shining from her pussy and his cock in hand. He positioned himself at her entrance and speared her in a long, hard thrust.

The feel of him gliding effortlessly to the hilt made her already powerful orgasm even more out of control. He stroked into her hard and fast, and she bucked with every thrust.

How could he do this? How could he make her so wild, so wanton? How could he clear her mind of everything except the feel of his hard member deep inside her? She couldn't think well enough to answer that question. All she could do was rock back into him as the fluttering in her pussy slowed and she went weak against the bed almost in the same moment that he grunted out a sound similar to her name and spent his seed inside of her in a hot spurt.

He collapsed over her, his arms tangling with hers as he drew her to her side and cocooned his body around her. She settled back against him, craving his warmth, reveling in the protectiveness she felt in his embrace. For the moment, that was all that mattered. For the moment, it was real...it was true...and it was hers.

Chapter Fifteen

Time seemed to slow in Miles' arms, so Portia wasn't certain exactly how much of it had passed when he pressed a soft kiss to her shoulder and rolled away from her to his back, separating their bodies with a grumble she echoed.

She took her time in facing him, always uncertain of what his expression would be. To her surprise, he seemed thoughtful as he stared at her through hooded lids.

"Did I please you?" she whispered.

He arched a brow. "Did my grunts of ecstasy and my utter lack of control in spending my seed not tell you the answer to that question?"

She blushed at his directness, despite the fact she had very recently been spread out before him for his taking.

"I don't know what to think of you, that is all," she explained. "I suppose, over time, I will become more accustomed to your expressions and be able to read their indications of your feelings."

He frowned at that statement, as if her growing closer to him was not an inevitability at all.

"You needn't get to know me a bit to know this, Portia." He stroked a finger against her cheek. "You satisfy me entirely. It was as if your body was made for my pleasure and being a part of your erotic awakening is almost magic to me."

Her blush returned, but this time for a different reason. His words, shocking as they were, were also very kind. It was something her life had lacked for a good while and she couldn't help but lean into it, into his hand to soak it up.

"I think this arrangement will suit us both very well," he continued, dropping his hand from her face and settling back against the pillows. "It turns out we are very compatible in the bedroom and since you have promised me surrender, I think that compatibility will only grow. But I must tell you something now, before we move further."

She looked up into his face. His gaze had darkened, it was unreadable, though his jaw was set like he was angry or upset.

"What is it?" she whispered.

He swallowed. "Our marriage will never include love, Portia. I feel I must clarify that for you so that we never have a situation where one of us is more attached to the other. It can only breed pain, and I would not wish that upon you."

She stared at him. Loveless marriages were common in their sphere, it was true. And given the circumstances of their arrangement, she had never expected him to fall in love with her. *Her* of all people.

And yet, hearing him say out loud, such a short time into a surprisingly passionate union, that he would never, *ever* love her...it stung.

She turned her face so he wouldn't see that tiny twinge of regret that shocked her and made her utterly foolish.

Her silence, though, seemed to say enough. He shifted to look at her even though she refused to meet his gaze.

"That should not be a difficult thing for you, should it?" he asked. "After all, you love another, don't you?"

She jerked her face toward him. "A-another?"

His brow wrinkled. "Ava's brother, Liam. When we met at the masquerade, you were looking for him. You admitted to caring for him."

She blinked. Liam. Good God, she hadn't been thinking of him at all as of late. Not for Ava's sake, certainly not for her own. And yet for years she had mooned over him, quietly lamenting the fact that he never noticed her.

Had she loved him? That didn't seem to fit, even though she might have owned it when pressed just a few weeks or months ago.

"Portia?" Miles repeated.

She glanced at him a second time. He was so devastatingly handsome in the dying firelight. His touch was so warm. He was so bent on her pleasure before his.

And he would never love her.

Worse, although she might not be able to fully read his emotions in every situation, she could plainly see that if she ever said anything to imply that she was capable of loving him...he might very well run.

So she found herself nodding.

"Y-Yes," she whispered. "I suppose I have always thought myself in love with him."

His gaze held hers for a beat too long and then he nodded.

"Good." He cleared his throat. "Then we shall not be fools, either of us, when it comes to matters of the heart. Though I would ask you to keep your feelings for him discreet."

"Of course," Portia croaked out, and her voice sounded very small and faraway over the rush of blood through her ears. "Despite the behavior somehow brought out by you, I would never do anything to embarrass you. Not—not again."

His expression softened. "I am anything but embarrassed, Portia. If you would allow me, I will take you somewhere tonight to prove it. And perhaps to press those boundaries you claim you are willing to allow me to test."

Portia swallowed. "Tonight?"

He nodded. "I promise you, if you agree, it will be very much worth your while."

Portia bit her lip as nervousness swamped her, erasing the pleasure which lingered in her limbs after his recent touch. But a bargain was a bargain, wasn't it? And she wasn't about to renege as she had seen her father and brother do over the years. She owed Miles that, she owed her mother that...she owed herself that.

"Very well," she whispered. "I will go where you take me, my lord."

"Yes," he said, his voice suddenly rougher. "Then if you will excuse me, I will ready myself and I hope you will do the same."

She nodded once as he slid from her bed and pulled his trousers up to refasten them. He tossed a quick, wicked grin in her direction as he moved to the door that connected their chambers by way of the sitting room.

"Portia," he said as he opened it.

She nodded.

"No chemise, please," he said, arching a brow before he disappeared into the other room.

Portia stared at the door, at the place where he had stood. Now that he was gone, she couldn't help but relive his comments about love. About the fact he would never feel that for her. And now her face fell as she hadn't allowed it to when he watched her so closely.

"Don't be an idiot," she muttered as she got up to ring for Bridget's assistance. "Love would be a ridiculous notion to pursue with this man and his reputation."

But even as she busied herself with wrapping a dressing gown around herself, her very reasonable words did little to comfort her. And little to ease the sting that still existed deep within her at her husband's dismissal of all matters of the heart.

Miles sent a side-glance toward Portia as they stepped up to the entrance of a pretty little middle-class home on the edge of London. A man stood there, dressed in a fine livery with a podium before him and a quill in his hand.

"Ah, Lord Weatherfield," the man said without prompting and quietly checked his name off a list. "And guest."

Miles nodded. "Good evening, Stenson. Nice to see you."

"It has been a while. Please do go in and have a refreshment."

Portia seemed confused as they entered the foyer, but she retained her composure, just as she always seemed to do. Until the first moan echoed from one of the several open doors that led into a parlor or other chamber.

She looked at him, eyes wide and bright with both interest and fear.

"Where are we?" she whispered.

He smiled. "A very fine establishment that caters to exactly the interest we both share in watching and being watched during certain acts."

Her throat worked as she swallowed hard. "Something like the Donville Masquerade?"

"Better," he assured her. "Far more selective and private."

She glanced back at the now-shut front door. "That was why he ticked your name off a list."

Miles nodded. "I am a member of this club and have been for years."

Her lips parted as she wet them and his groin clenched with desire.

"Miles, I wear no mask, people will see me, people will—"

"Never speak of anything, even if they do recognize us. Their membership in the club depends upon it, as do their own reputations in Society. Trust me, Portia. I do not throw you to the wolves by bringing you here tonight. I want to give you pleasure, not pain."

She seemed to consider that for a long moment as her gaze continued to dart around the staid foyer as if looking for more proof that this house of sin existed. When a second moan of pleasure echoed, this time from another room, her eyes fluttered shut on what was a sigh of desire so clear that it hardened him fully in a second.

"I trust you," she whispered. "And I surrender myself to your care."

"Excellent," he said, placing a hand on her back to guide her into the first room to their right.

She caught her breath and he looked around, trying to see the chamber through her innocent eyes. It was painted in a dark, sensual blue and the walls were scattered with expensive, erotic art depicting nudes reclining as they played with each other. Darker curtains had been drawn across the windows tonight for privacy from outside. Of course, some nights, when there were masquerades, they were opened exactly for the titillation of knowing prying eyes were on the guests.

Seats had been scattered about the room, all facing the small stage that had been erected along the long, back wall. Curtains were drawn there and already a few patrons had gathered for the show.

He steered her to a seat in the back, where they still had a clear view, but wouldn't be the center of attention. Perhaps one day she would be ready for that, but not yet.

171

"What is this?" she asked as she settled her shaking hands in her lap and cast a wary side-glance at the stage.

Before he could answer, the last few patrons rushed in to take their seats, the door to the parlor closed and the curtain swept open to reveal Madame Larouche, the owner of the home and club they now sat in. She wore a short, black, see-through skirt and a complex top that supported the bounty of her breasts but left them exposed for the pleasure of her audience. By the hardness of her nipples and the wet sheen of them, she had already engaged in some sexual play backstage.

Portia shifted beside him in both discomfort and interest.

"She—she is almost naked," she whispered.

He remained silent, allowing Portia her own reactions as music rose from an unseen pianoforte. It was a driving, passionate rhythm, and Madame Larouche began to move in time to it, using the entire stage as she arched her back, thrust her hips, created both delicate and lewd movements to simulate sex play.

As Miles watched her, Portia stared at the other woman. Her lips were slightly parted and her breath was shorter. He could tell from the high color on her cheeks that she was both embarrassed and titillated. He could only imagine how she would react when the next part of the dance began.

He smiled as he reached out to take her hand just as Madame Larouche's partner entered the stage.

The woman lived with three men, all her lovers both individually and as a group. At least one of them joined her onstage during her performances. Tonight it was the tallest of the three, a dark-haired man Miles thought was called Rowland.

He was utterly naked, his cock already hard as he moved over to Madame Larouche. He tapped her shoulder, then spun her around by the waist and drew her against him. Their lips
172

nearly touched but never met as he moved against her, lifting her effortlessly to slide up and down his body.

Portia jolted, her gaze sweeping over to Miles. "I—" she whispered. "I don't—"

"Of course, it is shocking," he murmured, turning toward her and sliding her chair closer so that he could whisper against her ear. "But look at how confident she is, how passionate. Does it not arouse you to see how he wants her? To see her body ripen and change as he glides her over his skin or lowers his lips to her throat?"

After he had asked the question, he brought his own mouth to the side of Portia's neck and began to suck there, gently.

She stiffened but leaned closer, her breath coming in faster gasps now.

Onstage, Madame Larouche and her lover continued to move to the music, but the dance was over. She dropped to her knees, positioning him so the crowd would have best advantage, and then sucked his cock between her lips. She laved her tongue over him as she looked up the length of his body to watch him.

Her lover thrust in time to the continuing music, tangling one hand in her thick hair to guide her movements for his pleasure.

Portia snuck another glance his way, first at his face, then a swift peek down his body to the hard cock that pressed against his trouser front. She licked her lips and then returned her attention to the couple onstage.

Desire lurched through Miles, almost out of control in its power. He put an arm around Portia and began to lightly strum one nipple through her thin, silky gown. She gasped but didn't pull away, arching against him as he plucked her sensitive flesh.

Onstage, Rowland dragged Madame Larouche to her feet, lifting her to wrap her legs around him as he carried her to a small settee on one side of the stage. He set her down, turned her and smiled at the audience before he speared her pussy with one long thrust.

Immediately she mewled in pleasure, arching back against him. Miles shifted, not thinking of the two fucking before him, but of taking Portia in much the same way just before they came here. He glanced at her. Her breath was coming in deep pants now and her nipple was hard as a diamond beneath her gown. How he wanted to suckle her, to glide beneath her skirts and pleasure her with his mouth as she watched.

Not today, though, not today. Not yet.

Instead, he leaned in close to her ear and whispered, "Don't just watch them—look at the others."

She jolted at the feel of his mouth on her skin but did as she had been told. She looked around the room with another catch of her breath. Some of the men had their members out, stroking them as they watched. A few couples were there in the room and one woman had her skirts lifted as her lover stroked her with his fingers and they moaned in time with Larouche and Rowland.

"Oh my God," Portia whispered.

He leaned in, kissing her neck. "Shhh," he murmured against her smooth skin. "Don't let your fear take over. Enjoy what you see. Imagine what will come from it later. Think of what it would be like to be that woman onstage, being taken for all to see as she cries out in ultimate pleasure."

She looked at Larouche. Her lover was driving into her hard now as she played with herself in earnest. Her orgasm was obvious as her head dipped back and she keened out a cry of pure pleasure, her hips thrusting back in demand of her lover's release. He obliged, coming almost immediately as the crowd

174

applauded and moaned in time. The curtain fell as the couple onstage finally indulged in a long, passionate kiss. Immediately the room began to clear, leaving Miles and Portia sitting alone.

She stared at him. "Why did they all depart so swiftly?" she whispered, her voice rough and soft.

He cleared his throat, taken aback by his own pulsing desire. "They moved to other rooms where they could take their pleasures."

"There is more?" Portia asked, eyes wide.

He nodded. "But not for us tonight. Right now I want you without prying eyes." He stood and offered a hand. "But we will come back here, Portia."

She seemed to consider that for a moment, but then nodded. "I-I want to see what else this place has to offer."

He swallowed hard. A woman raised with such limits, told she was not wanted, and yet her erotic nature survived and even thrived with only a little tending. How would she be in a month? A year? Five years?

He couldn't wait to see. But for now...

He pulled her to her feet and tugged so that she fell against his chest. He lowered his mouth to hers, burning his desire into her lips as he kissed her with all the passion the scene before them, and her reactions to it, had inspired.

"Come to my carriage. I cannot wait to get you home."

"Then don't," Portia whispered, giving him a look so filled with desire and passion that his cock actually twitched. She moved toward the door. "Your carriage door has a lock—why not have me right now?"

Portia couldn't believe her boldness, even as the carriage pulled up to the door and Miles hustled her inside without even waiting for help. She had never thought she would say something so out of character, but something in her had shifted as she watched that woman onstage with her lover. She had wanted to be so confident, so desirable.

And the words of lust had fallen from her lips without hesitation. But now the carriage door was closed, Miles was turning the lock and staring at her with undeniable desire in his eyes. She would have to follow through with her wicked suggestion.

But to her surprise, that thought gave her more of a thrill than a terror. She swallowed back hesitation and instead, lifted her hands to the buttons along the front of her gown and parted it in a matter of seconds. She pushed her arms free and sat across from him, breasts exposed, nipples still hard from his earlier touch.

"I want..." she began, thinking of all she had seen. There were so many delights to be explored, but one returned to her mind again and again. "I want to do to you what that woman did to her lover. I want to taste you."

Miles stared at her, this time his eyes filled with disbelief. She wasn't sure whether to be triumphant or concerned that she had silenced him so.

"Or do you not like the idea?" she asked.

His smile was one of a wolf in the hen house as he found the buttons of his trousers and loosened them so that his cock bounced free of the confines.

"On the contrary, Portia. I like that idea more than I could ever express to you in words."

He shrugged out of his jacket and laid it on the floor at his feet. She took the hint and knelt there, positioning herself between his legs. She stared at the hard thrust of flesh waiting for her. She had feared this, but now she craved it. She dreamed of it.

Slowly, she captured him in her shaking palm and stroked him from head to base. He hissed out a sound of pleasure and his teeth sank into his lip.

"Oh yes, just like that," he practically purred.

She was buoyed by the enthusiastic response, by the fact that he clenched at the carriage seat as if he had little control. She wanted that control. She wanted to surprise him and shock him and please him.

Since he had already declared this physical union was all they would have, she could only take every moment that was offered.

She lowered her mouth toward him, first gently rubbing the head of his cock against her lips. He was so soft and yet so hard, and she couldn't help but allow her tongue to dart out to taste him.

He let out a cry that said surprise and pleasure all at once, and she looked up the length of his body at him. He met her gaze, and his eyes darkened with wicked desires. Ones that spurned her on in her journey to take just a little of the confident control he always possessed.

She licked him again, this time with the full flat of her tongue. Again. Again. She tried to remember everything the woman at the club had done and slowly she fit him between her lips and into her mouth.

He was hot against her tongue, with a slightly sweet flavor she immediately craved more than any sweet treat she had ever consumed. She began to move over him, mimicking the motions of sex, taking him as deeply as she could manage. As she worked him with her mouth, she also continued stroking him with her hand, using her own saliva as a lubricant to make smooth, even strokes.

He arched his back, fingernails scraping the carriage seat, and swore beneath his breath.

Then suddenly he caught her beneath the arms and dragged her up his body to crush his mouth to hers. As he kissed her with wild, emotional abandon, he shoved at her skirts, finding her bare beneath her gown just as he had asked.

He positioned her onto his lap and she automatically shifted so that she straddled him, her sex stroking his cock before she took him deep inside with one hard thrust.

She gasped at the pleasure of this new position and immediately gripped his shoulders for purchase as she began to ride him. Every move was on impulse—she didn't think, but only felt.

The muscles of her pussy rippled as pleasure exploded inside of her without warning, without control, without anything except pure, unadulterated ecstasy. Her thighs clamped tightly around his and she arched as she moaned his name in the carriage. His driver could probably hear her, but she found she didn't care. She didn't care if the world could hear or see, she just wanted more of this pleasure, more of this exquisite feeling that rocked her body like lightning and made her feel more alive than she had before.

He clasped her hips, hard enough that the touch bordered between pleasure and pain and cried out, then she felt the spurt of his seed inside of her as he joined her in release.

She collapsed, trembling, her arms around him as their panting breaths merged into one. It was only the rumbling of the carriage that kept her grounded and aware that they were certainly in a somewhat-precarious position.

She pulled away and looked down at him in the dim light. Her emotions were so tangled. She was at once embarrassed by her boldness and buoyed by it.

"Why did you stop me in my pleasuring of you?" she asked. "You seemed to be enjoying it, or am I such an innocent that I misread the signs?"

He shook his head as he gently lifted her away from him. She shifted to the seat beside him and began the awkward task of dressing in a carriage. Without a maid. And with a very handsome man watching her every move.

"I liked it a great deal," he said, helping her with a few buttons. "Far too much. I would have spent before I pressed myself inside of you. And while there will be times I might allow such a reaction, tonight I wanted to pleasure you. After what we watched, I thought you deserved to come."

She smiled as she moved to the opposite side of the vehicle and stared at him as he now slowly fixed himself. Damn the man for being just as alluring putting himself away as he did stripping down.

"You tell me so often about what I deserve," she laughed. "As if you had made some great study of me when we both know that is far from true."

Rather than laugh or smile with her, his lips pursed. "Perhaps I did not pay close-enough attention to you before, but as my wife, I certainly am making a most detailed examination, much to your pleasure, I think."

Her smile faded at the flash of powerful desire in his stare. Once again, he seemed ready to pounce. And she found herself eager to allow that. To open herself to him and give him every inch of her body.

What a wanton that made her and how little she cared.

"Yes," she agreed as they pulled around the corner and into the drive of their home. "I cannot deny that I am most amenable to every attention you pay to me."

"Then it seems I have guessed correctly on what you deserve, what you need and what you desire," her husband said, offering a hand as the carriage stopped. "And I am willing to prove that once again, as soon as we are upstairs in our chamber."

Portia smiled as she watched him step down and allowed him to help her do the same. But even as she took his arm and followed him into the house, even as her body tingled with anticipation of all the pleasures to come, a tiny part of her resisted.

A tiny part of her that couldn't help but remind her that her husband's attentions only seemed to focus on her body's needs, which left her heart, her mind and her soul jealously waiting, and knowing that she would never be completely fulfilled.

Chapter Sixteen

"How do you keep your eyes from crossing when you do that?"

Portia laughed as she looked up from the needlework she was focused on and stared instead at her mother. Thomasina was reading, glasses perched on her nose and Potts safely by her side, laughing along with them.

"Perhaps they do cross—I cannot see myself," Portia teased, putting her handiwork aside with a contented sigh.

It had been over a week since Miles had taken Portia to his sinful little club, and in that time she had begun to settle into what was now feeling like home. And accepting her new life as well.

She spent her days learning the routines of Miles' house, fostering relationships with her very kind new servants and having final fittings for the gowns Miles had ordered before they wed.

It was a quiet life, peaceful, and she found she very much liked living here, being Lady Weatherfield, feeling safe for the first time in so long that she couldn't even remember it.

Between that and watching her mother relax, her episodes spreading out further and further, she could ask for nothing more.

And yet Miles provided more. The moment he was in a room with her, the sexual tension between them simmered. She was aware of him in every way, from the intoxicating scent of his flesh to the brush of his skin to the way his voice rumbled.

Her awareness of herself had grown, as well. She now knew what it meant when her nipples tightened, when heated wetness flooded her thighs, when she could scarcely catch her breath for looking at her husband.

He had taken her over and over, both gently and roughly, in every position, with wicked words flowing from his mouth, and with such tenderness that she had to hide her tears when it was over.

It was enough. It would be enough.

"Good afternoon, ladies."

She turned to watch the subject of her thoughts enter the chamber. Miles had been at meetings with his solicitor all day and she had not seen him since he pleasured her with his mouth before he slipped from their bed that morning, leaving her gasping for air.

She rose to her feet and walked to his side to press a kiss to his cheek. Fire lit in his eyes that told her it was only the fact that her mother and Potts were sitting by that he did not move that kiss to her mouth...and then perhaps to other places.

"We didn't expect you so early," Portia said, voice wavering a little as she stepped away to reduce his effect on her. "Have you eaten? I could ring for an early tea."

"I did eat," he said, settling himself onto the chair that was positioned beside hers. "So you needn't trouble yourself. I merely finished my business a little early and thought I would see what trouble you ladies had created for yourselves."

Portia laughed as she returned to her seat and held up her needlepoint. "We are sadly lacking in trouble, my lord."

"Unless you count the adventures in a book as trouble," her mother added, smile wide.

Portia's heart swelled at the expression. Her mother had created such a strong connection to Miles. She adored him and was always lighter when he entered a room. For that alone, Portia loved him.

The world screeched to a halt and Portia stiffened. Around her Miles continued his conversation with her mother and Potts, but Portia could hardly hear their words. She could only hear her own thoughts, echoing in her head.

Loved him.

No, that wasn't possible. Not in so short a time, not with a man who had already declared anything deeper than sex was impossible for them. Loving him would be disastrous indeed.

And yet, as she watched him with her family, those words rang so true. So deep. So painfully real.

"Portia?"

She blinked, clearing her mind of the realization that rocked her world, and forced a smile for Miles, who was staring at her, awaiting some kind of response to whatever he had said.

"I'm sorry, I was woolgathering," she said, her breath short. Would he notice the change in her mood? Would he be able to see her heart?

He frowned slightly. "I was only saying that the night will be very clear."

She nodded with relief. The weather was a safe-enough topic.

"Yes. It has been sunny today, despite the cold."

"So you shall have to dress very warmly," he continued, locking gazes with her.

She hesitated. "Warmly? I-I'm sorry I must have been lost in thought longer than I believed. Where will I be going that I will require warm clothes?"

He turned toward her. "I was telling your mother and Potts that you and I have been invited to a gathering at the Duke and Duchess of Laurelgreen's London estate and I have accepted."

Portia's stomach turned and she found herself scooting back against her seat, trying to make herself smaller.

"No," she whispered.

The entire room was now focused on her. Potts shook her head slightly, Miles stared and even her mother worried her hands in her lap.

"My dear," he said softly. "We are expected to attend these sorts of things."

"Not yet," Portia said.

Her mind flashed to brief images of eyes on her. Judging eyes that burned. Of whispers, unconnected snippets of ugly words like *madness* and *spinster* and *worthless*.

"Please don't force me to do this."

Potts cleared her throat and rose to her feet. "My lady, I believe we were going to take a turn around the rose garden to enjoy this rare winter sun, weren't we?"

Portia's mother stared at her daughter a moment longer, then got to her own feet with a nod. "Y-Yes. We shall leave you two."

The two women slowly exited the room, but not before Portia's mother placed a gentle hand on her arm and smiled weakly.

Now her mother was pitying her? She had sunk low indeed.

When they were gone, Portia pushed to her feet and paced to the window that overlooked the street. Outside people bustled about, not looking up at her, not even aware of her in her protective bubble of Miles' home. But once she left that protection...

"Portia," he said, rising to join her at the window. "We will have to face Society some time. You know that."

"Why?" she asked, turning toward him and hoping she had some strength to her face, rather than only pathetic fear. "Everyone knows the circumstances under which we were wed. Why cannot I stay in this house or your country house with my mother, away from it all?"

He shook his head. "Portia—"

But she refused to hear his protest. "No one would say a word to you about it, that you hid your unwanted wife away. You would probably be lauded by many for your good decision. And you and I would know the truth."

"The truth?"

She threw up her hands "That we get along, that we share passion. Does anyone else have to see us for that to be true?"

He held her stare a long moment, then reached out to take her hands. "I would no more relegate you to a prisoner in this home than I would allow your mother to be put into a madhouse. To do so would make me no better than your bastard of a brother."

Portia tugged at her hands, but he would not release them.

"You think you would be happy locked away, but you wouldn't be," he insisted.

"How would you know?" Portia asked. "You only know what my body desires, you know nothing of *me* and you have made it clear you never will."

He flinched at her peevish tone and tugged her a little closer. "I know you are a passionate advocate for your mother. I know you love Ava as a sister. I know you are kind to those who need kindness. I know you doubt yourself."

Portia tried to wave him off, tried to block out his words that burrowed into her soul, but he would not be deterred, and continued.

"I know that you would tap your foot to the music as you waited along the wall long before we were wed." He shook his head. "Portia, I know that whether or not you believe it, there is a part of you that would hate being cut off from everyone in our sphere."

She blinked. "How did you know I tapped my foot to the music at balls?"

He shrugged and let go of her hands. "I *did* notice you, Portia. You recall, I did come and ask you to dance from time to time."

She pursed her lips because there was no denying it. "Yes, you did do that."

"We are going to this gathering tonight," he said.

She parted her lips to protest, but he held up a hand to silence her.

"We *are* going. Ava and Christian will be there, my sister and Richard will also be in attendance, so you will not lack friends to comfort you. And I will stay at your side at all times."

Her brow wrinkled. "At all times?"

He nodded. "Yes. And I will make you a bargain. If, after we do this duty a handful of times, you still feel the same way, I shall banish you away and not ask you to attend anymore."

Her eyes went wide. "Never again?"

"Never," he promised.

She nodded. At least there was an option of hiding at some point. "Very well, then I shall attend. But I cannot promise you I will be a first-rate companion."

He smiled slightly. "I could picture you as no less, no matter what you say to convince me. Now come, why don't we join your mother and Potts for their turn about the garden?"

Portia went through the motions to take his arm and allow him to lead her outside into the brisk air, but even as she pretended to be comfortable, to be relaxed, her mind raced. Whatever Miles said, tonight would be anything but pleasant.

And she only hoped that seeing her at her worst, that his hearing the poor opinions of others, wouldn't damage the tenuous bond she and her husband had begun to forge.

The carriage crept through the icy London streets, busy with many who had taken advantage of a full moon to guide their rigs to parties, balls and other entertainments.

Miles let the curtain fall against the images outside and looked across the vehicle at Portia. She worried a handkerchief in her hands, staring at the fabric as she tugged it to and fro. There was no denying her resistance to going to this gathering was very real, couched in true fears he couldn't understand. Balls bored him; they did not inspire terror at the level she exhibited.

He reached out to cover her hand, and her gaze jerked to his. For a brief moment, he wanted nothing more than to comfort her.

"You will tear it in two," he said softly, removing the mangled cloth from her fingers and smoothing it in his lap.

She blushed but didn't reply, even as he began to fold it carefully. Her silence troubled him, so he chose a topic he knew would please her.

"Your mother has seemed to take to my home quite well," he said.

Just as he had expected, her expression softened and the anxiety left her face and body.

"Oh yes. She seems so much lighter there, so much more at ease. There was a minor episode yesterday morning when her tea was placed on the wrong side of her plate, but other than that, she is much improved thanks to your kindness."

He tilted his head as he looked at Portia. Yes, she seemed pleased, but there was more to it than that.

"You know, we have never spoken with much depth about your mother," he said, continuing to fold the handkerchief carefully. "She can be very attentive, so that you could never tell she suffered from any issues. But in the next breath—"

Portia shivered. "Everything changes," she finished for him. "That is how it has always been, I fear."

"Always?" he pressed.

She shrugged. "Well, at least as long as I can recall, though others have told me she was once very different. More able to control her troubled thoughts."

"Why did she change?" he asked and was surprised that he truly wished to know the answer.

She hesitated a moment, her gaze focused on her lap as she struggled.

"My father wanted her because she was beautiful," she began, her voice very soft. "And because she had suitors lined up to woo her and he wished to win the prize that all desired that Season. I suppose also because she came with a handsome dowry that would help replenish the coffers his bad gambling had emptied."

Miles drew back. Portia's father's gambling was well known before his death, but Miles had never heard how far back the origins went.

"Even then?"

She laughed, though the sound had no joy to it. "Always. He was compelled to give his money away, I shall never understand that."

"But he won your mother," Miles encouraged.

"Yes. And yet, just like so many other things he had won over the years, he lost interest in her almost as quickly as he wed her. She became a way for him to create his heirs and spares, nothing more. And with her sensitive nature, I'm certain it must have hurt her deeply to see his interest wane."

She turned her face away and he couldn't help but think of their recent conversation about love and the future of their union. How similar that must have seemed to what her father did to her mother and now Miles regretted not being more tactful.

"She bred him a son quickly enough, but then the problems began." She blinked as if to control tears. "My mother suffered the loss of child after child, and her state deteriorated with each one. And when she did birth again, it was me, a girl. My father was cruel. He blamed her, reminded her constantly that she was shirking her duty, potentially destroying his legacy. That constant strain broke her down even further."

"I had no idea he was so devilish toward her." Miles shook his head, filled with sudden anger at the past Portia and her mother had suffered...and the reminder of his own past. "Cruelty is the weapon of too many men, hidden behind closed doors while they pretend to be so true and decent to the world."

Her gaze lifted. "You sound as if you have personal experience."

Now it was his turn to tense with anxiety. The history he and Tennille shared with their violently abusive father wasn't something he had ever shared with anyone outside of their family.

And yet Portia felt like anything but an outsider now. He wanted to tell her, to let her know that he understood.

"My father—" he began, then stopped.

This was too much. It wasn't just a confession, but something more intimate. It would bind them in a way he had never allowed himself to be connected to a woman.

And even with this woman, it was too far.

"Your father?" she repeated when he was silent.

Her gaze was soft with understanding and empathy, but he ignored that and shook his head.

"Well, you know he died when I was young. And I don't think I ever lived up to his lofty expectations." That much was true, at least. "But I suppose most sons do not."

She nodded slowly, though she searched his face as if looking for more. Finally she moved to his side of the carriage and slipped her hand into his.

"We will do better," she whispered. "With our children."

He jolted at that statement. Of course there would be children, sometime in the future. Children who would be a hodgepodge of the two of them. Children he suddenly saw very clearly and longed to give the life neither of them had experienced.

"Yes," he said, unable to say more as those powerful images continued to bombard him.

She straightened up, her cheeks pink with as much discomfort with this topic as he felt. With a laugh, she pointed at the handkerchief, breaking the tension of the moment.

"You say that I was mangling that thing. What are *you* doing with it?"

He released her hand, ignoring the difficulty it was to do so and lifted the handkerchief. With a few more folds, he revealed he had turned it into the shape of a butterfly, complete with flapping wings when one tugged its little tail.

Wide-eyed, Portia took the item from his hand and balanced it on her palm. "Remarkable! Where did you learn such a thing?"

He shrugged, though her wonder at his little skill warmed him in ways he could hardly acknowledge.

"I have had occasion to interact with some performers."

She arched a brow. "A lover?"

"Long-ago lover," he reassured her, though he marveled at the fact she could point out his past indiscretions with no judgment or jealousy on her countenance.

"Well, if all the people we meet leave us with something, this pretty skill is certainly quite unexpected and delightful." She glanced up as the carriage slowed. "But now we are here, so I shall leave this on the seat so that it will surprise me again when we return."

He watched as she gently did just that, then drew a very deep breath to calm herself as they waited for the footman to open the door and assist.

He frowned. Was she right that every person one interacted with left a mark?

And if so, what mark would they leave on each other when their passion had faded and they became another loveless couple in the sea of Society?

Chapter Seventeen

Portia did her best to keep a smile plastered on her face, but Miles knew her well enough to see it was utterly false. There was none of her light there, nothing that said pleasure or joy since they had entered the ballroom.

Oh, she tried very hard to cover those things, but he saw her shrinking, easing into the wall, trying to be invisible. Her attempts were doomed to end in failure. After all, since their entrance to the party, no one had stopped whispering, staring and coming up to wish their felicitations, whether real or pretended.

He wanted to help her, but he had no idea how.

It seemed Ava was just as concerned, for she and Christian had not left them alone since their arrival. Ava watched her friend like a mother hen, concerned about a wayward chick in her brood.

Now she slipped an arm around Portia and smiled.

"You do look beautiful in that dress," she said.

Portia looked down at herself and waved a hand to dismiss the new clothes.

"Thank you." She shifted her focus to Miles. "When will be depart?"

He frowned. "We've been here but an hour, Portia. It is far too early to leave without causing a scene. A third of the guests haven't even arrived."

She turned her face away, lips pursed in upset. "Wonderful, more to look and judge."

"Why do they matter to you?" Miles asked, tilting his head so he could see her face more clearly.

She jerked her gaze to him with a shake of her head. "Because they all know you didn't want me, Miles. Because they are talking and judging with every breath that passes through their lungs. Because The Earl of Sandeford's wretched daughter Elinor has been glaring at me all night."

Miles wrinkled his brow. "Why would she do that?"

Portia gasped in what appeared to be frustration and rolled her eyes in Ava's general direction, as if he were an idiot for not understanding her meaning at once.

"Everyone *knows* she had her eyes on you," his wife hissed.

Miles drew back. He could not be included in that "everyone". Although, now that he thought about it, he had noticed Sandeford's extra attention in the last six months, and last Season Lady Sandeford had seemed to be in his way quite a bit.

He cast a quick glance toward the aforementioned Lady Elinor. She was tall and thin, with blue eyes narrowed to angry slits. She seemed to be all angles and frowns.

"I think I made a far better match," Miles said with a shake of his head.

Portia took a long step away from him, her lips pale and shaking and tears flooding her eyes.

"Do not mock me," she whispered, then turned on her heel and marched away from their group.

He stared, not fully comprehending what had just happened. But she was upset and that was all that mattered. He moved to follow, but Ava placed a hand on his arm and shook her head when he looked at her.

"Christian, will you find Portia and bring her a drink, preferably strong?" Ava asked with a brief smile toward the Duke.

He glared at Miles, but nodded once. "Of course."

Miles tugged his arm away from Ava as the other man left them alone and glared at her. "What is the meaning of sending your husband to comfort *my* wife?"

"In this moment, she wouldn't accept your comfort," Ava said with a sigh. "You must be patient, my lord."

"Patience is not one of my virtues," he grumbled.

She smiled. "I have heard very little spoken about virtue when it comes to you at all, except for virtue stolen."

He looked at her, uncertain if Ava was teasing or judgmental. But there was no anger in her stare, only concern for Portia that could not be hidden.

"A man has a reputation, yes, and mine has not been the best," he admitted.

Her expression softened. "I think I, of all people, know that one cannot be measured by reputation alone, my lord. Your actions toward my friend show that you are worthy of far more than has been whispered about you."

He pondered that a moment. "I appreciate that you think so, but it seems my wife does not."

Ava shrugged. "It is always hard to ascertain what Portia truly thinks or feels. She makes certain of that fact."

Miles nodded. There was no truer statement than that one. Their short time together had proven it.

He cleared his throat. "You know Portia better than anyone, I think."

Ava nodded and her smile widened. "Indeed, that is probably true. We have been friends for fourteen years. Since we were ten."

Miles considered that fact a moment and found a twinge of jealousy settled in his chest. Although he had known Portia longer, he had never cultivated a relationship like Ava's. Lady Rothcastle had seen Portia at her best and worst. She was allowed into his wife's heart in a way he had not yet found and perhaps never would, given the circumstances of their union.

"Can you explain to me why she has so little faith in herself, in others?" he asked.

Ava arched a brow. "You are asking me to break confidences, you know."

He pursed his lips. "I understand that. But I am her husband. I see her in pain and I want to ease that. I think, after every cruel way she has been treated, that she deserves it."

Her eyes narrowed at that explanation. "What you just said is the answer to your question, you know. Portia flinches away from others, from any faith in herself exactly *because* of the cruelty you describe. She has spent her life being punished for the acts and problems of those in her family."

He nodded. "You mean her mother, I suppose."

"Yes, that is the obvious connection, but her father's scandalous losses in the hells and her brother's equally dangerous drive to gamble instead of earn have not helped her. Nor has his dismissive treatment of her over the years." Ava's gaze grew distant. "In the beginning, when she first came out, people were especially cruel."

Miles tried to recall the year Portia had come out in Society, but found he could not. He remembered seeing her at balls and parties over the years, of course, of dancing with her when he felt the need to help...but he couldn't recall the pomp of her first Season, when girls were often celebrated.

He couldn't recall it because she hadn't been the least bit important to him.

Ava sighed. "Eventually the talk died down a little. She became just another hopeless spinster along the wall."

He flinched at the coldness of that reality. Worse, that he had been a part of it, looking at her, but never seeing the truth of her sensuality, her unusual beauty, her strength of mind and character.

"But now, because of the circumstances of your union, the world whispers about her once more," Ava finished, shaking her head.

"It reminds her of the past," he whispered.

She nodded. "I see it on her face, in her eyes, and it breaks my heart."

Miles rubbed a hand over his face. "Then how do I stop it? How do I help her?"

Ava drew back in what seemed like surprise. "Do you want to?"

He didn't hesitate. "Yes. Of course I do!"

A hint of a smile fluttered over Ava's lips, though he couldn't read whatever her thoughts were.

"I don't know how you could change their whispers. You two made quite a shocking splash and that will be talked about for a good long time to come. But you could change *what* they whisper about."

"What do you mean?" he asked.

"Right now people are talking about entrapment and unwanted brides," Ava said with a shake of her head. "They are pitying you and despising her for ruining your life and their chances at becoming your popular marchioness. Change that."

The facts hit him like punches to the chest. His life had always been so charmed, despite the painful past he hid from the world. In public, though, he had never suffered from a lack of friends, a lack of female interest. He had never considered those things might actually hurt his wife.

He nodded. "Yes, I see. Then I should go and find her."

He turned to do just that, but Ava caught his elbow. When he faced her, her expression was grave.

"I only ask that you do not give her something you intend to take away later, my lord," she said, her voice wavering just a little. "If a person is shattered enough times, they will become incapable of picking up the pieces."

She released his elbow and backed away. Miles stared at her a moment, then left her without another word, moving into the crowd to find his wife. But even as he maneuvered, unseeing, through the increasing crowd, he couldn't help but be very troubled by Ava's words. They rang too close to Tennille's comment that he could make Portia love him.

He didn't want that. And yet the thought of it was not entirely unpleasant as he moved toward the terrace where he was certain he would find Portia waiting.

Portia felt Christian staring at her, his kind gaze burning into her back as she leaned on the terrace wall, staring out over the gardens below. Slowly, she turned to look at her friend's handsome husband with as real a smile as she could manage.

"You have been most attentive, but Christian, you are not required to spend your evening with me, watching my every move like a hawk."

He arched a brow. "You think not? My dearest Portia, you are the closest friend my wife has and she loves you as she would a sister. Therefore, your happiness is hers and your heartbreak is hers. Because I love her, my job is to take care of anything and anyone that affects her so deeply. Consequently, it is *exactly* my job to stand with you and offer you comfort...or refreshment...or anything else that will aid you." He smiled and his stern face softened slightly. "Aside from all that, I like you and I hate to see you hurting."

Portia's smile because far more real at his words, but she couldn't help but feel the sting of them as well. Christian was living proof that a marriage born from a history of pain and despair could blossom into one of deep love, friendship and mutual respect. He adored Ava beyond measure.

And he stood there, a handsome, walking reminder of what she could never have.

"You are so kind," she said, trying to keep her tone even so he wouldn't hear the pain in her voice. "And I am so very lucky to have you and Ava in my life. But I need a moment to myself."

"Are you certain?"

She nodded. "Please."

His brow wrinkled, but he nodded slowly. "Very well, Portia. We will be just inside."

She watched as he walked away, but the moment he had gone into the house, she spun back to the terrace wall with a gasp of all the emotion she'd been keeping inside.

Her heart ached with humiliation and pain, and she could hardly bear it. She felt so...so...*foolish*. Foolish because she knew every person in that ballroom was fully aware of what a sham her marriage was, whether she found powerful pleasure in Miles' bed or not. Their passion didn't change the truth, it only made it more palatable when they were alone.

Behind her the terrace door opened, and she tensed, not wanting an intruder, good-intentioned or not, to be a part of this desperate moment.

But as the door clicked shut, something in the air around her shifted, grew heavier, and she knew, even without turning, that it was Miles who had come onto the terrace with her. Miles, the one man who wouldn't leave even if she begged. She felt his stare on her back, burning through her clothing, through her body to her very soul.

But he did not speak. Even as she kept her back to him, even as the moments stretched out.

Finally, she turned to face him. "Miles," she whispered.

He held out a hand. "Dance with me."

She blinked in confusion. That was the last thing she expected him to say and in the shadows of the terrace, she couldn't read his expression.

"What?"

He moved closer and took her hand to draw her closer. He was warm compared to the brisk winter air and smelled of pine and other masculine things. She couldn't help but think of his bare skin against hers, his mouth on hers, even in this tense moment.

"Come inside and dance with me, Portia," he repeated just above a whisper.

She shook her head, unwanted tears flooding her eyes. "Miles, I don't want your pity—" she began, but he cut her off by placing two fingers on her lips.

"It is not for my pity, it is for my pleasure," he insisted. "Come inside and dance with me."

She looked down at her hand in his, feeling the protective warmth of his fingers. With a shiver, she nodded and allowed him to lead her inside and through the crowd to where the orchestra had just begun to play the strains of a waltz.

Portia had danced with Miles a handful of times over the years. She had always been impressed by how graceful he was, how effortlessly he moved. Now that she had been in his bed, she could see that the act of sex and the act of dancing were linked, that he was proficient in one likely because of a high proficiency in the other.

He caught her around the waist with one firm hand and they spun into the crowd. She felt the eyes of the *ton* move to them immediately and had to force herself not to bolt from the room.

"Look at me," he said softly, as if he could read her discomfort. "Never take your gaze from mine."

She shuddered at the thought. As if that would ease her distress. It would only compound it when she was lost in his dark, swirling gaze.

But she did as she had been told and soon she forgot the other couples around them, she no longer heard their pointed whispers or felt their judgmental stares. All the world, all *her* world, was focused on Miles, and he gave back the same intensity as he received. For a moment she believed she was the only important woman in his life.

She swallowed as she tried to cling to some reality.

"I-I was never given permission to waltz," she stammered.

A foolish thing to say since it only reinforced her pathetic history, but it jumped from her lips anyway.

He smiled. "It is a good thing that as a married woman you can tell those biddies at Almack's to fly a kite. You may waltz with me any time. In fact, I insist that you do so any time there is an opportunity."

"Why?" she said, laughter escaping her lips despite her uneasiness. "I certainly cannot be the best dancer you have ever encountered in your long, illustrious career as a rake."

"Was it illustrious?" he asked with a grin that made her stomach clench with quick, unexpected desire.

"You know it was, you cad," she giggled.

"Well, I shall not debate a lady on the subject," he said, twirling her gently. "But I have found you are the only person interesting enough to share a waltz with. So I will repeat my insistence that you make yourself available every time the dance is to be danced."

The music faded and she slowly came to a stop and curtseyed playfully. "Whatever his lordship desires."

His smile faded, and he took her hand, raising it to his lips. He gently brushed them across her knuckles until she sighed with pleasure.

Then he released her and offered his arm. She took it, brought back to reality in that moment. Their dance had been so private, so intimate that she had all but forgotten the stares on them. Now they were back, but as they left the dance floor, she couldn't help but notice those stares had...changed.

Instead of judgmental, those around them now looked...*confused*. She couldn't blame them. Had Miles just claimed her on the dance floor? If she had seen their dance from afar, would she judge them to be a real and happy couple?

What a fallacy.

They reached the edge of the crowd to find Ava and Christian had been joined by Miles' sister Tennille and her husband Richard. Portia forced a smile, for she wanted Tennille to like her.

"Good evening, my darlings, I am so sorry we're late," Tennille said with a smile as she pressed a kiss to first Miles' cheek and then surprised Portia by repeating the action to her. "Don't you look beautiful?"

Portia glanced down. Everyone kept saying that, and she could admit that the expensive, perfectly fitted gown did flatter her, but did it truly make her pretty? She had never judged herself as such.

"Thank you," she finally managed to squeak out.

Tennille smiled. "But you must be thirsty after the dance—won't you join me at the punch bowl?"

Her husband immediately stepped forward. "I would be glad to fetch drinks for all the ladies."

Tennille smiled at him but waved him away with one hand. "And deprive me of the chance to gossip with my new sister? For shame, my love."

Everyone else laughed, but Portia couldn't help but tense. If Tennille wanted to speak to her alone, what would she say? She had been very kind so far, but that could easily change if she had done something wrong.

"Of course I would be pleased to join you," Portia choked out, sending a quick look to Ava in the hopes her friend would save her.

But Ava smiled broadly and instead slipped to the dance floor with her husband. Christian's limp from old injuries kept him from dancing much, but he did so from time to time, with his wife's encouragement.

Portia swallowed hard and jolted as Tennille linked arms with her and drew her away from their husbands. As they moved slowly through the crowd, her sister-in-law squeezed her gently.

"I must say, you and my brother looked very happy during the waltz."

Portia sent a side-glance to Tennille. "He is a fine dancer. I'm certain he makes any partner look vastly improved."

Tennille laughed. "Perhaps, but that was not what I meant." She nodded to a few ladies who smiled at her then looked at Portia with uncertainty.

She blushed at the pointed nature of Tennille's stare. "Then what was your meaning? I'm apparently too daft to guess it."

There was a crowd around the table with the punch, so Tennille stopped and turned toward Portia.

"I meant you looked *happy*. Your smiles and laughter and the way he did not remove his gaze from you tell me you two are connected."

Portia dropped her chin. Connected. Perhaps physically, yes, but he made it so clear that there could be nothing more to it than that.

"After everything my brother has been through..." Tennille began, then trailed off with a shake of her head.

Portia stopped worrying about herself and instead focused her attention on her sister-in-law.

"Been through?" she repeated, trying to picture whatever she could mean.

Miles had lived a rather charmed existence as far as she could see. He had lost his parents young, of course, and that obviously troubled him based on their brief conversation in the carriage. But he had never seemed to suffer or want for anything.

Tennille bit her lip. "He wouldn't want me to go into detail, and it is a tale a husband should tell a wife, no one else. But Portia, remember that sometimes scars are not where they can be seen by all. My brother has suffered...and I hope that you will keep that in mind if he says or does things that—" She stopped with a shake of her head. "I've said too much. I'm sorry."

Portia stared at her sister-in-law, but before she could say anything further, space opened at the refreshment area and the two women wedged their way into the crowd to take their punch.

But as they returned to their husbands and Tennille changed the subject to more benign topics, Portia couldn't help but wonder what she didn't know about Miles.

And if he had suffered some unknown pains, what more they had in common than a mere physical attraction.

Chapter Eighteen

It was after midnight when the carriage pulled away from the home of the Duke and Duchess of Laurelgreen and into the busy streets of London. It had been a hectic night and yet Miles felt strangely at peace as he sat, Portia tucked up against him, his arm around her and the silly fabric butterfly he had created earlier in the evening perched in her lap. Her eyes were closed, a tiny smile on her face.

Just that small expression made his heart swell with pride and pleasure.

"You survived the night," he murmured.

She opened one eye to look at him and the smile grew. "I did. Thanks entirely to you, your family and our friends. Somehow by the end of the evening, even the congratulations on our marriage were beginning to sound sincere. Perhaps I imbibed in too much punch."

He laughed, though he knew the humor of her self-deprecation hid a deeper discomfort with her place in the world. But perhaps that would slowly melt away as she felt acceptance from him and from those around her.

"You may have done just that, but I believe those in attendance *were* beginning to see that our forced match is a good one. You were magnificent and you look beautiful."

He slipped a finger beneath her chin and tilted her face toward his. She sighed just as his lips touched hers and he glided his tongue between them to taste her. She melted against him, her soft fingers weaving into his hair as she arched against his chest with a tiny moan of pleasure.

He drew back to smile at her. "Very nice, but you will have me losing control in this carriage...*again*...if you aren't careful."

She tucked her head back into his shoulder. "I recall the last time you lost control in this carriage, it was more than pleasurable for me. So your warning does not discourage me."

"Good," he murmured, stroking his hand along hers slowly.

It was a long ride and he was in no hurry now. He had all night to seduce and worship her.

She began to smooth her hand over his chest gently, tucking it inside his jacket to where his body warmth was trapped. He was about to lift her into his lap and drag her in for another, far more passionate kiss, when she spoke again.

"I had a very interesting, albeit brief exchange with your sister tonight," she said.

He shook his head. "One does not generally want to discuss one's sister when one is about to tumble his wife against a carriage seat."

Her eyes went wide. "Is that what you were about to do?"

He arched a brow. "Do not pretend that you didn't know, you were most definitely encouraging such an act."

"Perhaps I was," she mused, holding his gaze.

He could see she would not be deterred and he sighed. "Well, then we must get all talk about Tennille out of your system, mustn't we? What *very* interesting things did my *very* interesting sister have to say?"

Portia hesitated long enough that Miles' stare filled with alarm. Perhaps Tennille was unwell or the children had an issue or a thousand other terrors that clenched his heart.

"Portia?"

She shook her head. "I'm sorry, I was only trying to think of a good way to explain. You see, it wasn't what your sister said, it was what she held back that drew my interest."

"I-I don't understand," he replied, leaning back to look at her more closely in the dim carriage.

"She implied that perhaps there is more to your past that I should know about," she said slowly. "That you have suffered without anyone ever knowing it and that is why you understand my own suffering so well. Is that true?"

Desire left Miles in an instant, replaced with a roaring voice in his head that screamed at him to push away, to lock out, to make her stop. He had already decided not to tell her those intimate secrets and he now fought against her intrusion with all his might.

He ignored that voice, calming himself before he spoke.

"How ridiculous," he said, but he heard the strain in his own tone. Judging from Portia's softening expression, so did she.

"Is it?" she whispered.

"Of course," he snapped, pulling away and forcing her to straighten up so she wouldn't slump on the seat. "You have reminded me more than once that I have lived a very charmed life, haven't you?"

She tilted her head, her gaze boring into him as if she were seeing him for the first time. "Charmed for all to see. But there are things that happen behind closed doors that perhaps we never see."

He flinched. She was far too close to the truth now.

"You are being preposterous." He pushed to sit across from her in the opposite seat and folded his arms.

"Your mother and father both died," she mused. "How difficult that must have been."

He measured his breath with difficulty and glared at her. How dare she intrude upon his memories?

"Stop," he growled.

"Your mother died when your sister was born, didn't she? How old were you?"

"Too young for it to matter," he lied. "And you are invading a subject that is far too personal."

"You know of my mother's madness," Portia said with a shake of her head. "How much more personal could we go?"

"That is different," he insisted.

Her brow wrinkled. "How?"

He opened his mouth, but no explanation came. He could think of nothing to say. She didn't seem to require him to speak though, for she tapped her chin with a forefinger.

"No, I think it isn't your mother who troubles you, at least not enough to make your sister refer to it. It's something else." She shook her head. "You were a man when your father died. We talked about it tonight, but perhaps you miss him more than you let on."

Miles tensed and his teeth ground as nausea bubbled up inside his stomach. Her saying those things, implying his father was worthy stole all reason from his mind temporarily.

"Miss him? I could only wish he would have left this earth a decade before. If I had been more of a man, I would have killed him myself."

The harsh words echoed in the carriage and Portia flinched back from them, surprise reflected all over her face. He bit back a curse. She had forced his hand and he had lost control. That was something he never did. Ever.

"My apologies," he began, trying to temper his tone. "I should not have said something so harsh in your company."

She didn't respond for a moment, but then she slowly reached her hand out to cover his. "I assure you, I am anything but offended. Miles, I had no idea your relationship with your father was so strained. I'm sorry."

He shook his head. She truly didn't understand and he could easily accept her apology and distract her with kisses...but as he looked at her, her face open with compassion and acceptance, he again felt the strangest desire to tell her more. To explain what he had spent years pretending away.

"It wasn't strain," he found himself choking out with great difficulty. "To say a relationship was strained implies it could be mended. That it is filled with misunderstanding. That could not be further from the truth, no matter what I said to you earlier tonight. I lied to you then to cover up what I didn't want to share."

She covered his hand with both of hers now and leaned closer. "Then tell me the truth now if you can."

He shook his head. "My father brutalized us. I don't remember a time when his fist was not his preferred method of discipline."

Portia's lips parted. "Oh, Miles."

He shrugged, dismissive of something he could not dismiss. He could not forget. Memories that haunted him even as he pretended they did not exist.

"The worst part was that there was never any why," he continued, thinking back to those terrible days. "Do something wrong, expect a beating. Do something right, hope you wouldn't receive a beating. Do nothing, there might be a beating."

"Did your sister fare as badly?" Portia whispered.

He barely managed a nod, for that question brought him more pain than any other.

"Worse, sometimes. I both longed for school and dreaded it. When I was gone for months at a time, I was safe, but she was in his crosshairs. When I was home, I could at least insert myself between them."

One solitary tear slipped down her cheek, but Portia made no effort to swipe it aside. "You tried to save her."

"Tried, but more often failed than succeeded, I fear." He shook his head in disgust with himself. "*That* was why I ended my friendship with your brother, by the way. I could not imagine treating a sister the way he treated you."

She blinked. "I had no idea any of this was happening. I recall being very young and seeing you with your father. You were formal, yes, but I didn't sense anything more was amiss."

He sighed. "No one ever did. His lordship was very good about keeping his strikes where no one would see. Or if we did end up bruised in obvious places, we were sequestered away from the world until we had healed. Once I was locked in my room for eight weeks while my arm healed after he broke it."

She sucked in her breath and couldn't hide the horror and pity on her face. "You must have despised him with every fiber of your being."

He nodded. "I was seventeen when he died, and despite the fact that she was but fifteen, my sister and I celebrated by getting rip-roaring drunk on that bastard's best scotch and burning every portrait of him that hung in the country estate. Not one servant intervened to prevent it."

A ghost of a smile crossed Portia's face. "That must have been incredibly satisfying. I had never thought of doing such a thing with my own father's portraits, though our relationship was not quite as damaged."

"It was satisfying in a way, but it didn't erase the torment. My sister especially suffered. Even after he was gone, she sometimes woke crying, unable to be consoled. And when she

210

came out, I think she sabotaged quite a few potential matches. I've learned recently that her happy relationship with Richard was also one she resisted thanks to our father's legacy of violence. Thankfully, the man is persistent and she has the happiness she deserves now."

Portia nodded. "They do seem very well matched and vastly content together."

For a moment, there was silence and Miles could only hope they were finished with this subject. But then she tilted her head. "What about you, Miles? Do *you* have the happiness you deserve?"

He shook his head. "Of course. I have my freedom, I have money, I do as I please without answering to anyone."

She didn't seem particularly impressed. "Independence isn't the same thing, I don't think, as happiness."

Miles shook his head. "You sound like my sister now. She forever tries to convince me that there is benefit to answering to *someone.*"

Portia thought about that a moment. "I think I tend to agree with Tennille."

He laughed. "I would think you, of all people, would relish the idea of independence after everything you'd been through."

"Not being forced to beg for my every need is certainly quite refreshing, do not mistake my meaning," she agreed. "But, Miles, don't you want someone to care enough about you to have an opinion about what you do? A true friend, someone who sincerely loves you, will risk your wrath to give you their real opinion, even if it varies from your own and you do not ask for it?"

"I would prefer to be trusted to make my own mistakes," he said, voice unexpectedly tight as he tried to ignore the truth to her words. He needed no one. She couldn't seduce him into believing otherwise.

"All right, so you make your own choices. But once you have made them, I would think having someone by your side would be better." She shrugged. "But I have not experienced your past, I do not judge you for what you think is best. And what do I know of what lords desire, anyway?"

He examined her face closely. There was such a softness to her features, such a welcoming expression that he was warmed to his core even if he claimed not to want to feel such a thing. Telling her these deepest secrets should not have given him such relief, and yet it *was* a relief to whisper these darkest moments of his life. To admit he wished his father dead and did not mourn him. And didn't that prove her argument against complete independence?

He pushed the thought aside.

"If you think you do not know what this lord desires, you are a fool," he said, touching her cheek with the back of his hand. She leaned into it with a smile. "I desire *you* at present and we are about to arrive at our home, where I shall take you upstairs and prove that to you once and for all."

She smiled, though for a moment a tightness remained around her lips. But she covered it and nodded.

"I cannot wait."

As the carriage slowed, he took her hand, warmed by her soft skin, warmed further by her acceptance and ability to understand him. Only those emotional connections were ones he had denied for a long time. They were ones he would continue to deny no matter what she did.

He had to.

Portia sighed as she looked at herself in the mirror one last time. Bridget had helped her change into a gorgeous new nightgown that had only arrived for her that very afternoon. After arranging her hair in long, flowing curls down her back, the maid had left her.

The mirror had never been a friend. She had too often seen her flaws there rather than her strengths, but Miles kept insisting she was beautiful, and in the flickering candlelight, she saw flashes of something she could be pleased with.

And things that still made her blush, even after dozens of times in Miles' bed. The gown was made of a nearly sheer black fabric that draped across her curves and left little to the imagination. Lace covered her breasts, but the dark pink of her nipples wasn't hidden by the small scraps.

She shivered, turned away from the mirror and moved through the sitting room that connected their two chambers. At Miles' door, she hesitated. He was waiting for her through that door. And they would make love all night.

Only it would be different now. Not only did she know secrets of his past she doubted he had shared with anyone, but she had admitted to herself that she loved him, despite the folly of that feeling.

Everything had changed. Nothing would ever be the same.

With a deep breath, she opened the door and entered, but she hadn't gone three steps when she skidded to a halt. Miles was already on the bed, naked, his cock half-ready as he waited for her.

She could hardly breathe as she stared at him, perfection embodied in his rippling hard body and confident smile as he looked her up and down.

"I was pondering breaking down your door to find out why you were taking so long, but this was definitely worth the wait," he murmured.

Her eyebrows lifted. "You would break down an unlocked door?"

He laughed. "To get to you in that scandalous nightgown...most definitely." He crooked a finger. "Come here."

She was frozen in place for a moment as desire, anticipation and a swell of powerful love rushed through her. This man was hers, perhaps not forever, but for now. And he wanted her, needed her, possessed her in ways that had changed her forever.

He chuckled. "Do I need to come collect you?"

She shook her head. "Perhaps next time. At this moment, I need no encouragement to join you."

She moved toward him, trying to remain calm as he kept his gaze glued to her. She slid onto the bed next to him and cupped his cheeks, dropping her mouth to his for a long, deep kiss.

When they parted, he chuckled as he placed his hands behind his head. "The lady takes charge, I very much like that."

"Do you?" she whispered, dragging her hand down his throat to caress his chest with the tips of her nails. "Then I shall have to do more of it."

"Do that," he growled, watching as she let her hand slide down the taut muscles of his stomach. She peeked down his body. Her touch had brought him to full hardness, and she shivered as she wrapped her hand around his length and stroked him once, twice.

"I want to take you in my mouth again," she whispered.

His smile broadened. "I would like that. But I want to do the same to you. Would you allow me to help us both have what we desire?"

"Both?" she repeated, her forehead wrinkling. "How could we pleasure each other simultaneously?"

He chuckled and slid down so he was lying flat on the bed. "Face downward," he ordered her

She turned, her face close to his hard cock.

"Now straddle my chest." His voice was strained with desire and he moaned as she followed his directions. He pushed at her long gown, flipping it up around her backside so that her bare pussy was revealed. Then he caught her hips and dragged her back.

She gasped. She was practically astride his face and he could just...

She broke off the thought as he smoothed a hand over her sex and parted her to allow his tongue access to the weeping slit beneath. He stroked over her, sucking the tender flesh.

She caught his cock in her hand again and swirled her tongue around the head even as she marveled at his skills with his mouth.

She squeezed her eyes shut, trying to focus simultaneously on the way his mouth moved on her, in her, and the hard thrust of his pleasure that was there for her ministrations. Gently, she wrapped her lips around him and took him as deeply as she could into her throat.

He jolted beneath her, his mouth ceasing for a brief moment as he grunted. Power surged in her, merging with pleasure until it was all a spinning, intoxicating mix. She increased the speed of her mouth as she took him inside, and all the while he lashed her sex with his tongue, tasting her, forcing her driving pleasure, her hips grinding against him as he took her to the edge of release.

But just as she reached the pinnacle, just as she lost all control, he pulled away. She hardly had time to register a reaction before he flipped her onto her back, his hands beneath her hips to lift them as he speared her with the same cock she had just had in her mouth.

215

She jolted as her orgasm rocked her. He thrust slowly, grinding his hips, keeping his gaze locked on hers as he claimed her, took her, drew out her pleasure until it bordered on pain. She was lost in the desire, lost in him. She clenched her legs hard around his hips and reached up, cupping the back of his neck to draw him down. When they kissed, she tasted her own earthy essence on his lips and she moaned with the decadence of that flavor and the act that had caused it.

As her body jolted with increased pleasure again, he clutched her closer, groaning into her mouth as he spent within her and collapsed into her embrace. She wrapped her arms around him, smoothing her hands over the muscles of his back as they panted together.

Finally, he eased up to look down at her, his gaze unreadable in the dying firelight. He was speechless for a long moment, then pushed her now-tangled hair away from her face.

"I wish—" he began.

She tilted her head in surprise at the truncated words.

"Wish?" she repeated on the barest of whispers.

He hesitated again, then shook his head before he pressed his lips to hers and began the slow process of stoking the flames of desire anew.

Chapter Nineteen

Miles paced his bedroom, unable to sleep despite the fact that he and Portia had spent a passionate night exploring each other. He turned and looked at her, sprawled naked across his bed, a tiny smile on her lips as she slept. Immediately, his body reacted as it always did, twitching to life and making very clear its demands to be inside of her.

But something else reacted too. Emotions swelled within him. The same ones that had nearly had him making confessions of caring for her, wanting their union to be real, wishing he had noticed her years before and surrendered to the strange, intoxicating web she now spun around him.

Statements which he could never say to her. Not only did he refuse to feel such weak emotions, but they would be desperately unfair to her. If she put too much faith in a true future, he would hurt her. And he didn't want to hurt her.

This was his cock talking. He was enraptured by her innocent passions, by her trusting surrender, that was all. He needed a way to distance himself. To give her pleasure without muddying the waters of their marriage.

And there was one way to do it. One way to manipulate her arousal at watching erotic acts, at being watched while performing them. It would take her to the edge, it would push her over, but in the end it would be better for them both.

He nodded at himself in the reflection of the mirror above the small washbasin across from his bed, but the expression on his face was anything but pleased now that he knew what he had to do. He turned away and returned to the bed to curl his body around hers.

Tomorrow he would do what he had to do. Tonight he would pretend it wasn't the only way.

Portia smiled at her mother, who was chatting happily about a rare trip out to the park around the corner, but her attention was continually brought back to Miles. Although he had been passionate and tender with her last night, today had found him cold, distant and obviously avoiding her.

Was his hunger for her sated at last?

She swallowed past the sudden lump in her throat and forced herself to remain unfazed by the possibility.

"I'm so glad you are comfortable enough to go out, Mama. And that the cold didn't stop you from enjoying the afternoon," she said.

Miles cleared his throat. "Indeed. Perhaps next time Portia could join you."

Thomasina lit up at once. "Oh yes, I would love that. And perhaps you could come with us as well, Miles."

Portia watched him, saw a shadow pass over his countenance, saw him struggle to answer. Then he shrugged.

"If I had the time, of course I would join you."

Her mother didn't sense the shift in his mood, but Portia could hardly breathe as she watched her husband stare at his plate, eyes blank. What in the world had happened in such short hours to make him pull away?

What had she done...not done...what had she said or not said?

Or was he just regretting sharing his past with her because he didn't care about her enough to be so emotionally intimate?

As the servants arrived to clear the final supper plates, Miles pushed to his feet. "I have a bit of business to attend to, so I won't be joining you ladies for dessert and sherry. But I would like to speak to you a moment, Portia."

Thomasina smiled at the couple, continuingly oblivious to the tensions coursing through the room. "Of course. I will meet you in the parlor, my dear."

As her mother slipped from the room, Portia slowly rose to her feet and faced Miles. She tried to make her jaw strong, tried to keep her emotions off her face, though she feared she failed miserably. Her anxiety was just too high to hide it, especially from Miles.

"Have I done something to displease you?" she managed to croak out, determined to put the subject on the table before he did.

He started, then shook his head. "No. Not at all. Why would you think so?"

She swallowed, for his words were reassuring though his expression was not.

"Because you refuse to meet my stare," she whispered. "Because you have avoided me since you slipped from our bed in the dawn hours."

He jerked his gaze up and she was almost pleased to see surprise on his face rather than whatever torment was making him so pinched.

"A few days ago, you would not have been so bold," he said.

She shrugged. "Much has happened in that short time and *you* are changing the subject."

He shook his head. "I would like to address why I wished to speak to you in private," he said, waving off her question with one hand she now wished to swat.

"Very well," she said through clenched teeth.

"Tonight after ten you and I will be going somewhere."

Portia drew back. "Going somewhere," she repeated blankly. "What does that mean?"

He lifted his brows and held her stare. "What do you think?"

"One of your sexual adventures?" she asked. As worried as she was about the state of their union, her body fluttered at the thought of some kind of passionate, wicked interlude at his mercy.

He nodded, the motion very slow. "Something like that. I will ensure that Bridget knows how you should be dressed. Meet me in the foyer in two hours."

Her lips parted. "Can *you* not simply tell me what to expect and how to dress or behave?"

He seemed to consider that a moment, then backed away. "Ten o'clock in the foyer, Portia. I will expect you."

Without another word, he turned on his heel and left her standing in the middle of the dining room, staring after him, speechless, her stomach in a knot somewhere in the vicinity of her pounding heart.

She drew a few deep breaths and then exited the room to join her mother in the parlor. She forced a smile on her face as she opened the door and found her mother perusing a small selection of desserts that had been placed on the sidebar for them.

"Half a year in this house and I shall gain two stone!"

Portia looked at her mother's slight frame and laughed. "I would like that. And you should enjoy yourself in every way, Mama. You deserve it."

She poured herself tea rather than sherry and took a place beside the fire. As she sipped the steaming liquid, she kept thinking about Miles. His expression, every turn of phrase, his eyes that would not look at her...

"And you may lose a stone that you cannot afford," her mother said as she sat across from her daughter and frowned. "You are not having dessert and you hardly touched your meal. One cannot exist on one's husband alone."

Portia jolted at the directness and awareness of her mother's statement. She stared, but Thomasina was innocently spearing a bite of sumptuous cake with a fork.

"M-Mama!" Portia finally stammered.

"You needn't be so shocked. I wasn't always a batty old woman," her mother said with a sigh that belied the teasing of her tone. "I understand what it is like when one is first married to a handsome man. Luckily, it seems Miles is not so fickle as your father turned out to be."

Portia bit her lip. Right now she wasn't as certain as her mother.

"Miles is kind, he is generous, but we are not a love match," she said instead. "I would not be so foolish as to think our current circumstances will not change in a heartbeat."

Or that they already hadn't.

She shrugged. "All I can do is try to keep the man happy as long as I can and hope he remains true to his promises after that."

Her mother set her plate aside and clenched her hands in her lap. "Of course a wife's duty is to think about the happiness of her husband," she said slowly. "But, my dear, I encourage you not to do so at the cost of your own."

Portia shook her head in disbelief. Was this the woman who had been so cut off from reality and the world for the past few years that Portia sometimes wasn't certain she was aware of any of it? Was *this* her mother?

"Being here is good for you," she finally responded, her hands shaking in her lap. "I wouldn't endanger that for any price."

Now her mother's expression became worried. "Please don't make your decisions based on protecting me, Portia. I wouldn't want to see you follow my path, for it cannot lead to happy places."

She swallowed. "What do you mean?"

"I crushed everything I was while I tried to make happy a man who could not have cared for me no matter what I did."

Portia bit her lip. That did sound eerily similar to her own circumstances.

"But as you say, Miles is not my father," she argued. "So how do I honor what he desires without sacrificing myself in an attempt to force him to see me, to want me, to love me if he cannot or will not do so?"

Her mother shifted. "Give him what he desires if it makes you happy. But don't be afraid to say no if he takes you too far, if you feel he has forgotten to think of you and your needs." Thomasina reached to take her hand. "I didn't stand up to your father enough. I wish I had and I don't want you to say the same thing to your daughter in twenty years."

Portia squeezed her mother's hand gently. "Thank you, Mama, for your advice and candor."

Her mother shrugged. "I cannot always give it, I know, but I love you, my darling. I hope you know that."

Tears swelled in Portia's eyes and she dropped to her knees to hug her mother tightly. "I know, Mama. And I love you so very much in return."

They clung to each other for a moment and then Portia pulled back, swiping at tears.

"If ever a moment called for cake, I don't know when else it would be," she laughed as she spun to take a slice of the delicious confection.

Her mother joined in the laughter and for the next hour they spoke of far less troubling subjects, but deep in her mind, Portia couldn't help but revisit her mother's advice.

Saying no to Miles would never be easy, but she realized she might have to do it to save her heart and even her sanity.

Miles shot a glance at his wife as their carriage slowed to a stop in front of a tidy London home. Once again there was nothing shocking about the place. Nothing that would imply what happened behind its doors.

But already Portia looked nervous and had been worrying her hands in her lap for the past twenty minutes. He sighed. Their relationship had shifted after secrets shared and tenderness exchanged. Not for the better, perhaps, since awkwardness was now between them, as well as emotions better left unsaid and unfelt.

"Is every middle-class home in the city a haven for sin?" Portia asked with a nervous laugh that broke a small portion of the tension.

He shook his head as the footman opened the door for them. "Only the ones I take you to, but doesn't it make traveling through London more interesting as you wonder what happens behind each door?"

She pondered that for a moment before she nodded with a blush. "It does a bit. I never would have imagined."

"And it only gets better," he promised as he waved the servant away to step down himself.

He turned back to assist her and caught his breath. Above him, looking down, her hand outstretched, she was beautiful in an ethereal way. Her hair was like pale spun gold, her dark eyes wide and unreadable against porcelain skin.

But more than that, he saw her heart, her loyalty, her strength in the face of adversity. It was all there, written on her face for anyone to see who wasn't too fool to overlook it.

He wanted to own her, truly own her, body, soul, heart. He wanted, in that moment, to make her happy in every way for the rest of her days.

The shock of that realization made him rock back on his heels and stare until she tilted her head.

"Miles?" she said. "Are you well? You are very pale."

He shook away the treacherous, dangerous, foolish thoughts and instead helped her down. "Fine. Come."

He knew he sounded short, but he couldn't risk anything different as he turned on his heel and moved toward the house, with her trailing behind him. It was abominably rude and he couldn't stop it. Not without saying too much, not without her seeing everything because she was clever.

The door opened and the servant there nodded and motioned toward the staircase leading up and up. He reached back and took her hand at last, squeezing gently as he led her up to the second floor, then down a hallway to a chamber.

They stood at the closed door and he turned to face her. She was pale, shaking even though she was trying to hold herself steady.

He cupped her slender shoulders with his palms and stared into her eyes, even as he silently ordered himself not to get lost there, not to change his mind about the prudence of what they were about to do.

"I don't hear the...the moans like I did at the club," Portia whispered.

He nodded. "That is because there aren't many others here. This isn't a club, it is a private residence used for very special rendezvous."

Swallowing hard, she murmured, "Special."

He squeezed gently. "I will be here with you," he reassured her.

She hesitated, but then she nodded, giving him her trust. His chest swelled at that and he released her to open the door behind him so that she wouldn't see how much her faith meant to him.

He stepped aside to allow her into the chamber. She took one step into the large room, looking around in nervous anticipation, but then she stopped, frozen in place. She turned back to him with a shake of her head.

"Miles?"

He looked into the room, seeing it through her still-innocent eyes. Candles flickered all around, a fire burned merrily across from a large bed where two shirtless men stood waiting.

He took her hand. "Don't be afraid."

She tugged gently against his grip. "What is happening?"

"You have this idiotic idea that no one could desire you, that you were invisible before our circumstances forced me to see you for the desirable woman you are." He swallowed because the next sentence was suddenly impossible to say. "Tonight, these men will prove to you how wrong you are."

225

Chapter Twenty

Portia could scarcely breathe as she stared at Miles. She was going mad, that was the only explanation for what she had just heard.

"You want me," she panted, "to go to bed with those two men?"

He hesitated, then shook his head. "Not fully."

She blinked, frustration meeting confusion and shock. "What does that mean?"

"I would not want you to completely submit yourself, not until—" Miles cut himself off with an uncomfortable shift of his weight. "But they will pleasure you without...without penetration."

Portia's mind spun and her heart sank deep, deep into her stomach. Not until? Not until what, he was finished with her? Not until she had borne him a few unquestionably legitimate heirs? Not until he didn't give a damn anymore?

"And what will you be doing while this is going on?" she asked, clenching her teeth and trying not to allow tears to fall. "*Fully* penetrating some whore in another chamber?"

He shook his head and his eyes were wide with surprise. "No, Portia, of course not. I will be watching you be pleasured. And when you cannot take it anymore, they will leave and I will enjoy the fruits of their labor."

Portia leaned against the wall beside the door and tried to catch her breath. None of this made sense, but she had to focus. Think.

She looked at the two men who were apparently here to seduce her in front of her husband. She couldn't deny they were very handsome. One was dark blond, thickly muscled like something out of Viking lore. The other was a taller, dark-haired man, lean from work.

Neither one made her quiver the way Miles did, but she couldn't pretend they weren't attractive. And they were watching her with open, blatant interest that was reinforced by thrusting erections beneath both men's trousers.

Somewhere deep within her, a scandalous flame ignited. What Miles proposed was wicked beyond words. But what would it feel like to be the center of attention of not one but two strangers? Strangers with what appeared to be very strong hands.

She shivered and looked at Miles again.

"Why?" she whispered.

He lifted his eyebrows as if he were shocked at her question. As if every man offered his wife to other men and not a word was said about it.

"For your pleasure," he explained. "For mine."

"For yours," she said.

He wanted this. If she said no, the newly developed distance between them might only grow wider.

She sucked in a breath and stepped farther into the room. The two men, her temporary lovers, straightened up with welcoming smiles.

"Did I lie about her beauty?" Miles said from behind her.

She jolted as she awaited the answer.

"You did not," the taller man said with a smile. "In fact, she may be more delectable than you described."

Portia looked for the lie in his eyes, but she could see none. He did truly desire her.

She peeked over her shoulder at Miles. He nodded.

"Go ahead. I will put a stop to it when it is time."

With a shiver, she walked toward the smiling men. With everything in her, she tried to block Miles out, to surrender as he wished, but she could feel his eyes on her even as the dark-haired man took her hand and drew her to stand between them. She could feel the warm, sweet breath of the muscular blond behind her ear, and her body reacted with desire of its own accord. It was both thrilling and yet it felt like a betrayal.

"Do you have names?" she whispered as the dark man before her cupped her cheek.

"Call me D and he is R," D said. "It is easier than names, more anonymous."

She swallowed. "And what will you call me?"

The blond man behind her, R, wrapped a hand around her waist and drew her against his hard chest.

"Beautiful," he breathed.

She let her eyes flutter shut, indulging in sensation in the hopes she could end the war raging in her confused, heated mind.

R cupped her breasts from behind and her body fully tensed as he began to massage the sensitive flesh. Miles had insisted she go without undergarments again, and her thin silk gown was hardly protection against the touch. Her nipples hardened as pleasure began to ignite between her legs to spiral through her body.

In front of her, D cupped her neck and lowered his mouth to hers. His lips covered hers and she wanted to run. She had never been kissed before Miles and now another man's mouth on hers was strange. But he was skilled and her body once again betrayed her when her lips parted and she groaned as he touched his tongue to hers.

She felt hands on the buttons along the front of her gown and her eyes flew open. As he continued to kiss her, D parted her dress and pushed it from her shoulders, baring her from the waist up. He drew back and looked down at her, eyes focused on her flesh. A heated blush rushed through her and she had to force herself not to cover her nakedness.

This was what Miles wanted. She reminded herself of that over and over again.

"You truly are beautiful," D murmured as he leaned down, pressing kisses along the column of her throat.

Behind her, R began to rotate his hips against her backside, allowing her to feel the hard length of his erection. She shuddered at the feel of that combined with D's kisses, the way he lowered, lowered until his tongue swirled around her puckered nipple. He sucked and her knees buckled as she cried out and looked toward Miles.

He was slouched on a chair across the room, watching it all with an unreadable expression. She could see his body was aroused, but what did he *think* as he watched her? What did he *feel* when he saw her in this position with other men...strangers?

Strangers who were now working together to push her gown over her hips and away from her body, leaving her naked between them.

She blushed, dipping her chin so she wouldn't see their stares rake over her even though she felt every heated moment. Her emotions were so tangled she could scarcely understand them all. She was both aroused and embarrassed, she wanted more, but she also wanted to run and hide.

And yet if the two men sensed any of that, they did not slow their seduction. Slowly, D turned her so that she faced R and now it was his turn to cup her face and kiss her. He was more forceful than the other man, demanding with his tongue. She jerked her hands to his lower arms to steady herself and melted into the passion and promise of his kiss.

Behind her, D rained light kisses along her shoulders, stoking his fingers over her flesh before he tasted it. Along her spine, his touch was unexpectedly powerful and she broke the kiss to cry out with pleasure as he dropped to his knees and pressed hot kisses into the hollow just above her naked backside.

"So responsive," R murmured as he cupped her breasts together and stroked his thumbs over the distended nipples until Portia could hardly breathe.

"Very," D responded with a smile in his tone. "Are you certain we cannot have her, my lord?"

Portia turned her face toward Miles, eyes wide but too overcome by desire to be able to speak. He sat up straight and shook his head.

"Yes," he said without hesitation or question. "Our arrangement stands, gentlemen."

"A pity," R whispered as he slowly dropped to his own knees before her, his mouth dragging over her body. "But I'm certain we will both enjoy this greatly."

Before Portia could respond to or question what R meant, he urged her to stand with her legs farther apart and gently parted her sex. He rubbed his cheek against her thigh and then darted out a thick, hot tongue to tease her already wet and aching clitoris. Meanwhile, behind her, D did the same, but he instead parted the smooth globes of her backside and gently placed a wet finger at the tight, forbidden entrance to her bottom.

The two touches, so focused, so wild and illicit, made her knees weak and she had to lean on R to keep from collapsing on the floor. She felt utterly desired, beautiful, erotic as the two men gently tasted and teased her.

And yet these wicked moments were nothing compared to how she felt when Miles smiled down at her as he slowly pressed his cock deep within her. Or the feel of his arms around her after they made love all afternoon and then lazed in the drowsy warmth of his bed.

There was no denying that these two men were talented lovers. And if she offered herself to them, she would be given powerful orgasms, she would be gifted physical pleasures that would curl her toes.

But there was more at stake than that now. If she did this, she would never be able to take it back. It would color every exchange with Miles for the rest of their years together. It would allow him to believe she was happy being a sexual plaything only, someone he could pass to some other man when he was finished with her and feeling guilty.

Even as pleasure mobbed her, she remembered her mother's admonishment not to tend to Miles' happiness at the sacrifice of her own.

There was only one thing to do. No matter how hard it would be.

With difficulty, she pushed R away and stepped to the side to extract herself from the powerful embrace of her would-be lovers. She dropped to pick up her dress and lifted it to cover her nudity as she shook her head at the two men.

"I'm sorry, I can't do this," she whispered. "You are both so very talented and your touches make me quiver, but I...can't. I simply can't."

The men exchanged a look of disbelief as they both stood, then stared at Miles in question. He rose to his feet and ignored them to focus on her.

"Portia?"

She shook her head, meeting his stare evenly although it was difficult. "No, Miles. I *won't.*"

His lips parted and then he said, "Gentlemen, you are excused."

It took a moment for the two men to gather their shirts and step out, but Miles never stopped staring at her the entire time. She couldn't tell if he was angry or disappointed or grateful or pleased. Only that he stared and she refused to allow that to intimidate her or change her mind.

Once the men had gone, the door closed behind them, Portia stepped into her gown and swiftly buttoned the front to cover herself.

"Would you care to explain what just happened?" Miles asked her softly.

Portia pursed her lips. There was a part of her that wanted to be totally honest with him. But if she said everything in her heart and mind, she would surely destroy what they had between them. She wasn't certain she was willing to do so.

"As I said, I simply did not want this," she whispered.

He cocked his head. "Did they not please you? I can find others who—"

She turned toward him, holding up her hand to stop him. "They were skilled, Miles. I'm sure I would have had enough orgasms to please you. Release had nothing to do with it."

He flinched. "I arranged this for your pleasure as much as mine."

She shook her head before she slowly crossed the room to take his hands. She looked up into his eyes, lost as always, filled with a love she desperately wished she didn't feel.

"Your experiment did make me feel desired, Miles. It made me feel beautiful and I appreciate the effort. But I do not want to go to bed with any other man."

He didn't react. Not even a blink. He only withdrew his hands from hers slowly.

"What about Windbury? *Liam.* You told me you loved him, you must wish to express that physically. Perhaps I could—"

She flinched. He certainly wished to be rid of her.

"Miles, I don't love Liam."

He shook his head. "You told me you did, Portia."

She sighed. "I won't deny that as a girl, I did harbor hopes, or fantasies, really, that Liam would notice me, *see* me, fall in love with me even. But Miles, I don't think of him."

Miles turned away from her unexpectedly. "You must."

She touched his arm and forced him to look at her again. "Not even a little, except to wonder if he will ever try to repair his relationship with Ava. He is the brother of my best friend and was kind to me as a child, so I will always care for the man and hope for the best for him. But I realized very swiftly after our scandal that I do not love the Earl of Windbury. I likely never did."

He was silent for far too long. "No?"

"No," she repeated, tears welling in her eyes. "But there *is* someone I love."

He shook his head. "Don't, Portia. Please do not say it."

"But I must," she said, touching his cheek. "So that you understand me. So that you don't mistake me ever again."

"If you say it, it will change everything," he warned her.

She hesitated at the wildness in his stare, at the caution of his words. And then she shrugged.

"Perhaps change is not the worst thing one can endure." She drew a deep breath. "There is only one man I want in my bed, my heart or my life, and it is you. I love you, Miles."

He flinched and her heart ached, but she continued regardless.

"And that statement does not come with expectations or demands because you have never promised me anything, you wouldn't be that cruel. But it is a promise that if you need me, I will always be there for you. And an explanation of why I will never, *ever* want any other man, no matter what reason you give me for why I should. You are the only one, you will only ever be the only one, for the rest of my life."

Now that the words had been spoken, Portia waited for the regret that would follow. But even as Miles stood there, silent and sick, she felt none. She *wanted* him to know her heart. And now he did.

"The proper reaction to this is a response of some kind," she said when he had been silent for far too long.

He nodded. "Yes, indeed that is likely so." His voice was thick. "I-I will send you home in the carriage."

She swallowed at the paleness of his countenance and the thinness of his lips. There was not an ounce of pleasure in him at her confession.

"And where will you go?" she managed to whisper with great effort.

He didn't answer, but motioned for the door. "Come. The carriage is waiting close by. It will take but a moment for it to be brought for you."

She bit back tears as she followed him from the room and downstairs where he murmured something to the butler who nodded and left them alone. Alone and silent as they stood side by side, but never touching while they waited for the carriage.

Finally the vehicle pulled to a stop in the circular drive and Miles led her down and helped her in. But as he moved to close the door, she inserted a foot to stop him.

"Miles," she whispered, reaching for him and cupping his face. "I'm not sorry I told you, even though I know it will destroy everything. But love is meant to be shared, and I would have regretted it more had I never confessed what is in my heart. I hope one day you will come to understand that, even though you'll never return those feelings."

He stared up at her, face crumpled with defeat and sadness.

"Goodnight," she added.

She let him go and pulled the door shut herself. And it wasn't until the carriage was safely on the road, heading toward home, did she let tears of disappointment fall.

Chapter Twenty-One

Ava was silent, her lips pinched and thin as she watched Portia pour tea. She had been silent for a very long time. Christian, however, was not.

"What do you mean your husband hasn't been home for three days?" he asked, repeating the last words Portia had said a few tense moments before when she told a sanitized version of her final encounter with Miles.

Christian was angry, there was no mistaking that. Portia flinched at the reactions of her friends. Here they were, happy together after a long battle to become so, and they couldn't understand what was happening in her life. But standing in their parlor, enduring their pitying stares, she could hardly explain her position either.

"I knew the risks of my confession of love when I made it," she said with a sigh as she leaned back in her chair. "And I cannot regret being truthful."

Ava blinked, her face filled with wonder. "You are forever filled with surprises, my friend."

She shrugged. "I didn't come here for pity. My mother has been anxious the past day and Potts thought I should go out and stop fussing over her."

Ava shot a glance at Christian that was filled with unspoken communication. He nodded, then he leaned over to press a brief kiss on Portia's cheek.

"You will never have my pity, my dear. Only my friendship. Now I shall go so you and Ava can discuss whatever it is women talk about when a man leaves the room."

Portia smiled weakly. "Boxing and the state of shipping."

He laughed as he kissed Ava and slipped from the room, leaving the two women alone.

The moment the door shut, Ava arched a brow. "Are you trying to tell me you aren't heartbroken?"

Portia shivered as emotions she had been ignoring ricocheted through her. Her eyes stung with tears and her hands shook before she clenched them in her lap.

"Of course I am heartbroken. I told Miles I loved him and he put me in a carriage and disappeared into the night and God knows whose arms." She shrugged. "I die a little every night when I wait for him and he doesn't come home. If I hadn't heard from some sympathetic servants that he was alive and well, only staying in another property he owns in London, I would fear he was dead."

Ava shut her eyes. "I'm sorry. It was a silly question."

Portia regained her composure with great difficulty. "I can only do my best to accept my current circumstances, can't I? I knew what the risks were when I said what I did. In fact, I could have avoided that confession altogether."

"And why didn't you?" Ava asked softly.

Portia shook her head in frustration. "I've spent my entire life hiding, trying to please men who didn't care about me. I said yes when I meant no, I kept quiet when I should have spoken. I hid against walls and prayed no one would look at me. All the support Miles has given me since our marriage showed me that I cannot do that anymore. I shouldn't. And so I was brutally honest with him. Perhaps that is the best I can be with *anyone* in my life."

Ava slipped over to the settee beside her and wrapped an arm around her. With a gasp of breath, Portia rested her head on her friend's shoulder.

"Anyone who doesn't love you is an idiot," her friend whispered. "You are remarkable."

Portia smiled through renewed tears. "Hopefully, I will someday feel that way. Right now I feel rather sad and empty despite my lack of regret."

"You *will* feel happy again, I assure you," Ava promised, though Portia couldn't believe her. Life wasn't fair sometimes, that was all there was to it.

The question was, could she learn to live with circumstances as they were now?

As Miles sat in the comfortable chair beside the fire at his club, he ached as if he'd been in a physical fight with a person twice his size. But as he stared at the half-empty drink in his hand, he couldn't deny it wasn't a physical pain that damaged him so deeply.

It was something far more intense and disturbing.

He wanted to go home. No, not just home. He *wanted* his wife. The wife who had told him she loved him with words that echoed in his mind on a constant loop, even in his restless dreams.

Only he couldn't do that. He couldn't face her and her feelings. He *couldn't* because it would only bring them both pain.

"Who knew you were such a son of a bitch."

Miles jolted as Christian, the Duke of Rothcastle, thrust himself into a chair across from him, set his cane aside, folded his arms and glared.

Miles sighed. So Portia's protectors had finally come for him. Good, he deserved whatever poison they would hurl his way.

"Rothcastle," he muttered as he poured himself another drink from the bottle he had pilfered from a servant at the club. "Would you like one?"

The duke shook his head. "I don't want your hospitality or your liquor, Weatherfield."

Miles leaned back and set his drink aside untouched. "Then have you come to challenge me to a duel?"

For a moment, Rothcastle seemed to consider the possibility.

"I would, but I doubt my wife would approve. She would tell me that killing you would bring Portia no pleasure, nor would it help her reputation. And unlike you, her *husband*, we actually care what happens to her."

Miles flinched. How he wanted to lash out at Rothcastle for saying such a thing. But he deserved it.

"I do care for her," he protested, rubbing a hand over his face. "What is happening between us is...it is very complicated, I wouldn't expect you to understand."

Christian leaned back with a snort of utter disgust. "Complicated? Complicated."

Now Miles was beginning to get angry. The mocking tone was beginning to grate.

"I don't ask you to take my side," he growled.

Rothcastle laughed. "Oh, and I don't. In fact, I have no sympathy for you whatsoever. You call your situation complicated? Ava and I had a family war between us and a dead sister I was bent on avenging no matter the cost." The duke's gaze became distant and pained. "I hurt that woman to the bone and she still loved me even though she lost her brother by doing so. *That* is complicated, my friend."

Miles was stunned into silence. Rothcastle never spoke of what had separated him and Ava, though everyone knew it. Now seeing both his pain and his love for his wife, Miles was ashamed.

Christian shook his head. "The only thing that stands between you and Portia are barriers you create for yourself because you're too cowardly to knock them down."

Miles stared at his drink again. "I'd be no good for her to love," he muttered.

Christian shrugged. "That may well be true. But you don't get to decide that for her. To do so would make you no better than her brother or her father or a dozen others who have stuffed her into a corner her entire life and stripped her of her right to control her own destiny."

"And what if I do worse?" he asked. "What if I am incapable of giving her what she needs or asks for?"

"Then you become capable," Christian said with a shrug, as if that were the easiest thing in the world to overcome. "I have seen you two together. Perhaps it was only a few times, but even in that limited capacity, I could tell you want to give her joy, happiness, strength. You seem to recognize what no one else could: her value. Is that not love?"

Silence was Miles' only reply, mostly because he couldn't think of another. Rothcastle was so frank and matter-of-fact that his words began to sink below the surface.

"Or perhaps I'm an idiot after all," the duke added with a shrug. "Perhaps you will be like every other rake in the kingdom and whine and moan about what you can and cannot do and can and cannot feel and you will lose a chance to be truly happy. It would be a loss for you both, but Ava and I will be there to pick up the pieces...once you settle Portia *very* handsomely, that is."

"I would do no less if I wasn't going to be there." Miles glared at the other man, but Christian seemed unfazed by any of it. "She wouldn't have to depend upon the kindness of friends or strangers. I would never allow her to fear her position again."

"How noble." The duke's tone was so dry it would have withered leaves. "But you continue to avoid the only answer that matters in this 'complicated' situation."

"And what is that?" Miles snarled, glaring at Christian.

The duke didn't seem to give a damn. "Do you love her or not?"

Miles' jaw set at the direct question the other man wasn't going to allow him to avoid. His mind spun with images of Portia, from her strength at every ball to her masked appearance at the Donville Masquerade, from her nervousness at their wedding to her surrender their wedding night. He recalled her sweetness, her kindness, her empathy and her courage. Even when she admitted she loved him, it had been with the full expectation that he would turn away from her.

And she did it anyway so that she could live her life with honesty and integrity.

He squeezed his eyes shut, hoping to block out emotions swelling within him. But it didn't help. There had been a dam he built long ago and cracks were forming, the flood was coming.

"You said you hurt Ava," he choked out. "She lost her brother to love you."

Christian flinched and nodded. "Yes."

"Don't you fear she will regret loving you? That one day you won't be worth the sacrifice?"

The other man's jaw set and he straightened his shoulders. "I do my best, every day, every moment I am with her, to be certain that I *am* worth anything she has lost. I respect her choice too much to do anything less. And as much as I wish I could strike you for the pain you have put my friend through, I think you may be capable of the very same thing. *If* you love her."

Miles slowly pushed to his feet and Christian looked at him in surprise. "And where are you going?"

"To talk to my wife," he responded as he smoothed his jacket. "I really don't think you should be the first person to hear what I need to say, do you?"

Christian chuckled. "Only if it's the right thing. Good luck, Weatherfield."

Miles nodded as he hurried from the club. He was going to need luck, now more than ever.

Chapter Twenty-Two

Portia took a deep breath to prepare herself as she stood on her stoop and forced a light smile to her face. The servants were likely gossiping like mad belowstairs; she refused to let her behavior give them even more fodder. It was the best she could do for what was left of her dignity.

When she was ready, she swept through the front door into the foyer and found Armstrong hustling to greet her.

"Good afternoon, my lady," he said, reaching out to take her wrap, gloves and hat. "I hope your visit found Her Grace well."

"It did indeed, thank you," she responded and the warmth of her smile became more real.

How she had ever feared Armstrong, she didn't know. The man was nothing but kind and accommodating as she learned her role as mistress of this house.

A role she hoped Miles wouldn't force her out of anytime soon.

She pushed the thought away and focused instead on the household items that needed addressing.

"Have you talked to Mirabelle about the butter situation?" she asked.

Armstrong cast a quick glance up the stairs, but then nodded. "Yes, my lady. It was a mistake in the ordering and it has been corrected with many apologies."

"Oh great God, please don't tell me she cried," Portia said with a frown. When Armstrong shifted, she threw up her hands.

"Well, send her to me after tea and I will reassure her myself. Accidents happen."

"Yes, my lady."

She moved into the parlor with him trailing after her. "My mother and Potts, how are they?"

Armstrong looked toward the stairs again, and she frowned. He was so distracted, certainly she hoped it had nothing to do with her mother's behavior of late. While she was better, a short spell of safety and content didn't erase decades of serious concerns.

"Armstrong?" she said, her voice sharper than perhaps she would have wished. "Nothing is wrong with my mother, is there?"

He shook his head, his attention snapped back to her, at least for the moment.

"No, miss. She and Miss Potts took a turn around the garden today that seemed to calm her considerably. She is resting now and Potts has gone to pick up a few things they ordered at the milliner last week."

"Oh dear, yes, the milliner." Portia smiled. "I cannot wait to see what they have concocted in the hat arena. If I am not immediately available when Potts returns, do have her fetch me for a demonstration."

Armstrong swallowed, his face very pale, and Portia tilted her head. "Good Lord, man, you are very out of sorts. Is there something amiss?"

He took a deep breath. "No, my lady. It is just that…"

She raised her eyebrows to encourage him when he trailed off in discomfort. "That…?"

"Your brother is here."

Portia froze and her head began to pound even harder than it had been all day. She didn't speak, but rubbed a hand over her face. "He is, is he?"

"He arrived half an hour ago and demanded he be allowed into a parlor to wait. He seemed intoxicated, despite the early hour." The butler smoothed his jacket. "I wasn't certain how to proceed, so I placed him in the green tea room."

Portia swallowed hard.

"I could have him removed, if that is what you would like," Armstrong continued.

Portia thought about that. It was exactly what she would like, but that would be the cowardly way to deal with a most unpleasant circumstance. If she was willing to be direct with her husband, perhaps it was time to be the same with her brother.

"No, I will see him. Though it might be best if you keep a few footmen at notice just in case he becomes unruly."

"Absolutely, my lady." The butler tilted his head. "They will be there to wait in moments."

"Thank you." She squeezed the other man's arm gently and then walked down the hallway toward the little tea room. Outside, she drew a long breath and then entered the chamber.

Her brother was not seated, but stood at the fireplace, hands clenched. When the door opened, he turned toward it, and she shook her head. He looked terrible. His face was puffy with drink and lack of sleep, his eyes dull and rimmed with red.

"Great God, Hammond," she said, pulling the door almost fully shut behind her, but not quite. "You look a sight."

He glared at her. "Impertinent chit."

She ignored the nasty tone and words. "You didn't send word you would be visiting today."

He shrugged. "I felt like coming, and you need me now more than ever, don't you?"

She wrinkled her brow as she slowly took a seat and stared up at him. "Need you?"

"Your husband has run off," he sneered, pleasure lighting up his gaze. "It's the talk of London."

Of course it was. Portia barely bit back a sob. "I don't know what my marital circumstances have to do with you, Hammond."

"When he puts you out, you and Mother will need a place to go, won't you? If you make certain he settles you well, if you make sure he gives me more blunt, I can ensure that place will be provided."

She barely held back a humorless bark of laughter. "I don't think I like the kinds of hell holes you pick out, Hammond."

He glared at her even more darkly, though he seemed to be having trouble focusing.

"How long did it take you to gamble away every penny he paid you to protect our mother?" she whispered. "You've had the money so short a time, but the desperation I see on your face tells me it must be gone already."

He flinched. "Shut your mouth, you stupid girl. We aren't talking about my failings, but yours. You'll need someone to take responsibility for you once he puts you on the street, so you'd best be nice."

Portia considered that charge. She might have believed it once, but now...

"You are so convinced that every person is as cold and cruel as you are," she said with a sad shake of her head. "But you don't know Miles. You don't even know me."

"I knew no man would want to keep you around more than a month, and I was right," he barked.

She didn't react, even though his words cut her more deeply than she would have liked.

"Miles may not love me," she began, the words sticking in her throat. "He may not even want me anymore, but he is a good man. A decent man. He would never leave me to your devices. He would never abandon me or our mother, even if he hated me. So I don't *need* you, Hammond."

His face darkened with anger and he moved on her a step. Now she did flinch and pushed to her feet to avoid any attack he might make in his drunken rage.

"You owe me!" he growled. "And by God, you will pay or I'll make sure you suffer for it."

She stared at him, this empty shell of a man who had been trained to hate by their equally empty shell of a father. She no longer feared him—she only pitied him. But she had no intention of ever allowing him to control her again.

"You have no power anymore," she said, surprised by how strong her voice sounded, even though it was quiet. "I have a higher title, I have far more money and I have people willing to put you out on your ass in the gutter if I so much as glance toward that door. So you may threaten, Hammond. You may bluster. But you will never hurt me or our mother again. And if you try, I will bring down the full force of my new resources upon you, is that clear?"

He stared at her, blank-faced and seemingly confused. "But you...but I..."

"You will leave here," she continued. "And you will never darken my door again. Never. Do that and I will consider making some kind of arrangement for a *small* stipend for your living expenses."

His lips pursed. "You would do this to your brother, your own flesh and blood?"

She shook her head. "The only reason I consider giving you anything is because you *are* my flesh and blood. Otherwise, you would have *nothing.*" She motioned to the door. "Now get out. If you don't, my men will come and assist you in leaving."

Hammond gaped. "Portia—"

She pointed to the exit more strenuously. "Good day."

He swallowed, then all but ran past her and out into the hall. Portia stared at the spot by the fire where he had stood as she heard him exit the front door without so much as a word for Armstrong.

"That must have felt very good."

She spun around to face the door, to face the voice she knew so well. There, standing in the entryway, smiling at her, was Miles.

How could he be so handsome, even more handsome than she remembered? He hadn't been shaving, apparently, so his face was scruffy with whiskers that gave him a rough, powerful look. His eyes were dark and bright with high emotions as they locked onto her and did not move.

"I—" she began, staring at him, drinking in the vision of him back in their home. Feeling such love for him that it hurt her chest.

"Portia," he murmured.

She swallowed hard and did her best to maintain a little dignity and control. "Miles, I-I didn't expect you home."

He frowned. "I'm sorry to have been gone for so long. I had a great deal to think about. I didn't expect to find your brother here. He hasn't troubled you while I've been absent, has he?"

She fought for breath enough to answer. "No, no, this was the first day he arrived. How long were you standing there?"

He smiled again as he entered the parlor and drew the door fully shut behind him. "Long enough to hear you stand up for yourself. Long enough to be so very proud of you."

Her heart swelled. "I thought that if I had decided to live my life with honesty, it had to extend to everyone, even my bastard of a brother."

Miles' smile fell ever so slightly at her mention of honesty. There was no doubt he was thinking about her unwanted confession of love for him.

"My favorite part was when you told him you would bring down the full force of your title and money on him if he troubled you again."

She blinked. Dear God, she had said that. "I hope you didn't think I overstepped, as it is your money and title I referred to."

"You may have both to bring Hammond down to size any time you need them."

Portia swallowed hard. They were talking so naturally when a wall was between them, so high she knew it couldn't be breeched. He shifted slightly and she knew he felt the same. He had come home for a reason. And she could see he had something to say.

She could only hope her face was calm and not reflecting the screaming fear and pain that lived inside of her as she anticipated what words would next fall from his mouth. She feared she already knew them.

He would tell her that he couldn't live with her if she loved him. That she would have to go away to another property and live as his wife in name alone. He might even say that he pitied her for her foolishness.

That would be the worst thing she could think of.

"Please sit," Portia said, motioning to a place before the fire and moving to the opposite seat. "We might as well be comfortable in body if we cannot be in spirit."

A ghost of a smile turned up his lips and he did what she asked. For a moment, they merely sat together, and Portia shifted in discomfort as he kept his stare focused intently on her.

"I want to talk to you about what you told me a few nights ago," he finally began.

"I understand." Her voice sounded so far away and funny, as if it belonged to someone else.

He took a deep breath. "Are your feelings the same now that we have had distance between us? Or have you reconsidered what you told me in what was, perhaps, the heat of the moment?"

She squeezed her eyes shut. He was giving her an opportunity and it would be so easy to play off what she had said and perhaps save some version of their arrangement. Instead, she nodded.

"Miles, my feelings are the same. I love you," she whispered, her voice breaking just a little.

He released his breath slowly, as if he had been holding it. "Then you and I need to discuss some new terms to our understanding."

"Our marriage, you mean," she whispered, bowing her head at his choice of words.

He nodded. "Yes, our marriage. Portia, you know my past."

She jerked her gaze up in surprise, for that was not the topic she had thought they would discuss. "Y-Yes."

His gaze grew distant. "You are the only person who knows it outside of my own sister. You have been exceedingly kind and understanding about my history, but you cannot be blind to the fact that it informs my future in many ways."

Portia was still confused about this line of discussion, but she nodded regardless, happy for the intimacy of this subject if nothing else.

"Of course it would," she said. "Our pasts shape us."

He flinched. "Well, my past makes it impossible for me to promise you that I know how to...how to be a good husband or friend to you, or even a good father to our children."

She drew back. "You have already been a good husband and friend to me."

He rolled his eyes. "Yes, trying to make you take two men as lovers, putting you into a carriage when you refused and ignoring you for three days is stellar behavior in a friend, you are correct."

She smiled gently, despite the sensitivity of the subject. "It might not have been your finest hour, but I never thought you did any of that out of cruelty, Miles."

His brow wrinkled. "Why *do* you think I did it?"

Her lips parted and she struggled to find the right words. "I-I believe you were taken aback by my admission of my feelings. I believe that since you do not feel anything like that for me that you were uncomfortable, not only because I violated a rule of our original arrangement, but also because you hesitated to strike down my hopes by telling me you will not and cannot ever feel the same way for me. Which is a noble thing in its own way."

"That's not why," he whispered, his expression gentling as he reached out to take her hand.

It was the first time he had touched her since that night they parted and Portia had a hard time not sighing with pleasure, with relief.

"Then why?" she managed to choke out.

"I left because I'm a coward." He dropped her hand and got to his feet to pace the room. "Because when you told me you loved me, it frightened me."

"Frightened?" she repeated in surprise. That was the last descriptor she ever would have thought he would use.

He nodded and when he spoke again, his tone was choked. "I don't want to be my father, who abused his family with his fists and his harsh words and his utter lack of compassion. But I don't know how to be better. I'm afraid I would let you down, Portia. I'm afraid I won't know what to do to make your life as beautiful as you deserve if you sank so low as to love me."

He bent his head in what seemed like defeat.

"I'm afraid I will regularly fail and disappoint you. And that one day you will look at me and regret you told me you loved me because your feelings have changed."

Portia blinked. This could not be happening. This confession wasn't the gentle dismissal she had been expecting. It was something else.

Something that gave her a thin reed of hope to cling to as she got to her feet and moved toward Miles slowly.

"I can guarantee you, Miles, you *will* fail me. I'm *certain* you will disappoint me." When he looked at her, his face was filled with pain, and she rushed to continue. "And *I* will sometimes do the same to you on both counts. If you live with and love someone long enough, they are bound to hurt you with what they say or do or don't say or don't do. But I won't regret any love I feel for you because if we were to stay together, to be together, those years would be filled with moments where we surprised each other, aided each other, brought each other joy and comforted each other through heartbreak. That is life, Miles. And it's love."

He scrubbed a hand over his face.

"So you are saying it is all a risk and all a reward?" he asked.

She smiled. "Absolutely. But, Miles, you needn't make yourself worry so. I know you don't love me. I didn't tell you that I loved you in order to extract some kind of promise or empty vow from you. I wanted you to know where I stood, but I never expected anything more. If you still wish to continue as we have, then wonderful. I will take that time you offer and cherish it. But if you are too uncomfortable—"

"I am very uncomfortable," he interrupted, looking her straight in the eye.

She stopped and tried to smile through the heartbreak. "I understand."

"No, you truly don't," he said with a humorless laugh. "I'm uncomfortable with the idea that you believe you know what is inside of me. That you think you can read my thoughts and yet you are so far off the mark."

Her brow wrinkled. "What do you mean?"

"I took you to spend the night with those men because I wanted to push you away," he said, shaking his head. "I *felt* something that night after the ball. Telling you about my past triggered emotions I had believed for years I was incapable of experiencing. I didn't want them and I thought that if I raised the level of our erotic games that somehow I could reset everything."

"I don't understand," she whispered, her breath short and her heart pounding loud enough she almost couldn't hear her own words.

"I will say it plainly. I'm telling you that I have fallen in love with you too," he explained.

The words all but echoed in the room, and Portia swayed as they bombarded her. She searched his face for the truth and thought she saw it there, but it couldn't be real.

"You are trying to be kind," she began.

He stopped her with a hard shake of his head. "On the contrary," he said with a shaky laugh. "I feel that offering my love to you is more cruelty than kindness, for I am a bad prospect and will hardly deserve you. But I will strive to do so every day for the rest of my life."

He reached for her and drew her close until she was wrapped in his arms, looking up into his handsome, worried, beautiful, amazing face.

"I love you, Portia. And if you are willing to put up with my failures, I will promise to love you and protect you and guard you and be a friend and lover to you for as long as we both draw breath."

Tears began to stream down her face, but Portia was too caught up to even make an attempt to swipe them away.

"Is this real?" she asked, cupping his cheeks. "Am I dreaming?"

He lowered his lips to hers and kissed her, filling her body with heat. She clung to him, drawing him even closer as he tasted and claimed her with his mouth.

Finally, he pulled back just enough to whisper, "Do you think you're dreaming now?"

She nodded with a laugh. "Absolutely. A dream come true. And I hope I never wake up."

About the Author

Jess Michaels is the award-winning author of over forty romances, erotic romances and urban fantasy novels. She lives in Arizona with her fantastic husband and two adorable cats. While not writing about sexy gentlemen and wicked ladies, she can be found doing geeky things like playing video games and performing aunt duties to two nephews. You can find her online at http://www.authorjessmichaels.com, on Facebook (Jess Michaels) and on Twitter (@jessmichaelsbks).

An eye for an eye, a sin for a sin...

Taken by the Duke
© *2013 Jess Michaels*

The Pleasure Wars, Book 1

Amid all the lies and scandals that fuel Society's gossip mill, one truth has stood out: House Rothcastle and House Windbury have always hated each other.

Lady Ava Windbury prays the feud will someday end, to no avail. One dreadful night, her brother accidentally causes the death of Christian Rothcastle's sister, a tragedy that leaves both men maimed.

Consumed by grief, Christian makes a grim decision. He will kidnap Lady Ava so that her family will feel the pain of loss as keenly as he feels the loss of his own sister. But once he has Ava in his clutches, desire takes unexpected hold. Even more surprising, she willingly surrenders to his every sexual whim— after haggling over the terms of giving up her virginity.

Too late, he realizes she is using her body for peace, not war. But just as their affair of revenges turns into an affair of the heart, the past rears its ugly head to take matters into its own hands...

Warning: This book contains scenes of erotic seduction, sexual revenge and the healing power of love.

Available now in ebook and print from Samhain Publishing.

Enjoy the following excerpt for Taken by the Duke:

Ava wasn't sure what Rothcastle thought of her, if he was drawn in by the façade of toughness she was currently pretending. But inside, she shook like the final leaf on a dying tree.

This man was...utterly intimidating, not only because he was her enemy or her captor, but because he had an air about him that screamed dark and dangerous. Not to mention, he filled the entire room, he sucked out the air around them, he crowded into her even when he was nowhere near her.

But still, she refused to show him his effect on her. Or at least, she *tried* not to show him.

He tilted his head to examine her closer and suddenly his expression changed slightly. He no longer had rage on his countenance, but something else just as powerful existed in his stare.

She had seen a flash of it before, in the carriage after her kidnapping, but had dismissed it as ridiculous. Now it was far clearer. He was...

He was *attracted* to her.

She might be an innocent, and even a wallflower, but she had been pursued enough as a young woman and seen enough other women pursued to know when a man liked her, even wanted her on some level. And the Duke of Rothcastle, her family's greatest, most terrifying enemy, had *desire* in his eyes when he looked at her.

It wasn't an attraction that was entirely unreturned. The first time she saw him, over eight years ago, was at a large garden party in London. She'd only been fifteen, not yet out, and she had looked across the croquet field to find a young man watching her. His bright blue eyes had been so beautiful that she had felt a sudden and strange urge to go to him.

In fact, she might have even moved to do so...until Portia told her it was Rothcastle. At twenty-three, he had already been duke for six years. Why she hadn't recognized him, she didn't know, except that she had been kept out of company most of her life. And thanks to her brother and father's tirades, in her mind she always saw Rothcastle as a monster, not a handsome, stern young man with stunning eyes.

But that was a very long time ago. And the desire he might feel for her now was nothing but a means for her to help her brother, or at the very least escape this pretty prison. She could not be so foolish as to feel a fluttering in her belly when he looked at her like that.

"Well?" she asked and her voice sounded funny, for she had not spoken for what seemed like an eternity.

"Terms," he said, his own voice rough as his gaze flitted up and down the length of her body. Now his desire turned darker, and her knees went slightly jelly and difficult to stand on. "Yes. I believe we might be able to come to terms."

The tone of his voice did not give her any joy, but she lifted her chin and refused to shiver. "Such as?"

"Because he hides like a coward in your estate in London, I cannot reach your brother to force him to repay the debt as I would see fit," he all but growled. She opened her mouth to argue that point, but he held up a hand to silence her. "But *you* could repay it on his behalf."

She could hardly breathe. "H-How?"

He looked her up and down a second time, predatory and feral. "With your body."

She blinked. That erased any doubt that he wanted her, although no gentleman spoke this way to a lady. To an innocent. Though she was an innocent who had heard things and read things. She wouldn't count herself as a shrinking flower by any means.

"My body," she repeated, letting the words roll from her tongue slowly. "I suppose you mean my innocence?"

He flushed and hesitated before he spoke again. It was almost as if he was battling with gentlemanly instincts she assumed he did not have to dare entertain such a shocking request—nay, demand.

"Yes," he finally said, his voice gravel. "Your innocence. And more."

Ava wanted to respond. Her sense of propriety told her to refuse his insulting request, to lash out at his shocking lack of decorum.

Another part of her, though, a deeper and darker part of her, had questions. She just didn't know how to phrase them since she could not fully picture this man taking her innocence, taking *more*, as he put it. And yet the stirrings in her body as she tried were anything but unpleasant.

"I have shocked you," he said with a faint smile. "Which is to be expected. It has been a long day, and I am certain you long for a bath and bed as much as I do. I will have a tray sent up to you with supper later. And we will discuss our 'terms', as you put it, tomorrow at far greater length."

Ava swallowed, still trying to find something else to say. Except she could find no words, and Lord Rothcastle was moving on her. He stepped closer, closer, until he filled her entire scope of vision.

"But you must have something to think about, some point of reference while you consider my offer," he murmured, low and utterly seductive. "So..."

He slipped a finger beneath her chin and tilted her face toward his. She could hardly breathe, she couldn't think as his mouth descended and suddenly his lips were on hers.

The pressure was gentle at first, compensating for her shocked stillness in response. But as she relaxed, her eyelids fluttering shut and her hands coming up to touch his forearms almost against her will, the kiss changed. He slid his hand into her hair and angled her face differently. His tongue slid out to dart along the crease of her lips, and she found herself parting them to allow him the access he asked for.

He delved inside and tasted her. Her world exploded around her into sparkling rainbow fragments. In that moment, as he explored her mouth with his warm, rough tongue, her knees went weak, her body seemed to melt and strong, powerful sensations of pleasure unlike anything she had ever known or felt ripped through her body.

A moan echoed on the air and she realized, quite to her shame, that the needy, wanton sound had escaped from her unruly body. And the moan only seemed to spurn Rothcastle on further. He tugged her closer, gentleness replaced by wild, animal intensity. She was crushed to him, her body molding to his as the kiss deepened, deepened. She was lost in it, and she feared he might be too.

She had no idea where it would have gone. She never knew, for there was a rap at the door that brought reality spiraling back. He all but shoved her aside, wiping his mouth on the back of his hand before he turned and called out, "Enter."

The uncomfortable butler from the foyer pressed inside. He spared Ava a quick glance and then inclined his head. "Lady Ava's rooms are ready, as is her bath, Your Grace. Yours has also been drawn."

Rothcastle...*Christian*, for now she could not help but think of him by his given name...turned toward her and his face was hard again. No sensuality remained. "I hope I have given you something to think about, my lady. Please follow Sanders. We will speak tomorrow."

He walked away, out the door and past his servant. Ava stared at the place where he had stood and all but made love to her with his mouth. Then she somehow gathered her composure and made her way to the waiting Sanders. But as she followed him up the stairs, she was keenly aware that her body was different now. The Duke of Rothcastle had awakened something in her with his searing kiss.

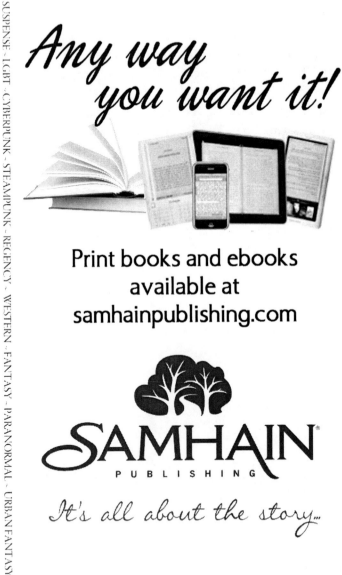

It's all about the story...

www.samhainpublishing.com

CPSIA information can be obtained at www.ICGtesting.com
Printed in the USA
LVOW11s2129130815

450012LV00002B/239/P

9 781619 222052